"Don't swim in the lagoon. It's infested with moray eels—and they're worse than sharks...."

That was one of the first things that Colonel Hugh North was told when he arrived at Fort Winfield on the island of Sanga Sanga.

North did not give the warning much thought. After all, he had not come to this forsaken Army post to swim. He was looking for a killer.

And now North stood at the edge of the lagoon, looking down on what was left of a human body. A woman, an officer's wife.

In all his years, North had never seen a corpse so horribly mutilated.

Why, everybody asked, had she gone into the lagoon when she knew about the eels?

And then Colonel North made a quiet, blood-freezing statement. "You know," he said, "she was murdered by a human hand."

*   *   *   *   *   *   *

THE SULU SEA MURDERS was first published by Doubleday, Doran & Company, Inc., many years ago. This is a completely rewritten and very substantially changed version of the earlier adventure story.

Other books by F. van Wyck Mason

F. van WYCK MASON

THE SULU SEA *Murders*

AN ABRIDGED EDITION

WILDSIDE PRESS

An earlier version of *The Sulu Sea Murders* was published in 1933, under the same title, for The Crime
Club, Inc., by Doubleday, Doran & Company, Inc.

THE
SULU SEA
MURDERS

Chapter One

COLONEL HUGH NORTH, United States Army, G-2, Criminal Investigation Division, was in Manila when the word was flashed to him straight from the Pentagon. The message shouted its drop-everything urgency despite all its involved code.

George Lee, key aide to spy Arnulf Hansen, released by Chinese Communists at Shaowu twenty-third last month. Lost in Hong Kong but reliable information says his destination is Zamboanga. Intercept and place under triple-A security. As if to add a row of exclamation points, the message ended with the cry, *Top priority.*

North's first reaction was a muttered, "Lee *would* pick Zamboanga in this season."

"Did you say something, Colonel?" Lieutenant Kenny Trotter asked brightly. Lieutenant Trotter was North's aide, pilot, good—if fledgling—right arm. He was a brash, blue-eyed youth who possessed a deep reverence for Colonel Hugh North that he masked under a humored camaraderie.

North's brown eyes were somber, his wide mouth was tightened at the corners as he studied the message, his memory casting back to the Hansen spy case. Twelve years was a long time in this speeded-up world, and some of the details were hazy, but the main fact had never dimmed: Arnulf Hansen had been the most successful (or most black-hearted) spymaster operating in the Philippine area before Pearl Harbor, and, unless G-2 was very wrong, some of his well-tutored agents were still in business. But not on Japan's payroll, these days.

So there was a chance at long last to learn who Arnulf Hansen's operatives were and who might still be in the dirty business, eh? George Lee, the only known survivor of the *Kinshu Maru*, was finally out of the Commie prison, available for questioning, was he? And hotter than a three-dollar pistol, for sure, if any other members of Hansen's old gang knew he was out and where he could be found.

Speaking of hot, the message from Washington had definitely mentioned Zamboanga. Hugh North groaned audibly.

"What's cookin' that distresses you so, Chief?" Kenny asked, against a thousand orders never to call North "Chief." "What tidings from the banks of the Potomac?" Trotter's round face caught the look in his colonel's eye as North turned, and the pilot's college-sophomore features sagged.

"Don't tell me we're pulling out!" he wailed. As

2

North nodded, Trotter gloomed, "Wouldn't you know! Just when I was starting to make some time with—"

"A gentleman never mentions the lady's name," North said primly, "and, besides, she'll keep. We're bound for Zamboanga."

"I see," Kenny said. He nodded wisely before he asked, "And just where is Zamboanga?"

North half shut his eyes to visualize a map. "We're in Manila," he said. "Okay, so we fly due south over Mindoro and Cuyo and Cagayan and Cavili, down the middle of the Sulu Sea, then south-southeast toward Sibuguey. At the southwestern tip of Sibuguey, on the Basilan Strait opposite Borneo, you'll find Zamboanga."

"I hope," Kenny Trotter added.

"Oh, you'll find it," North said. "If we get lost you can just lean out of the aircraft and find out the direction the hot draft is coming from. That will be Zamboanga, the hottest place in the world at this time of year."

"I am probably the worst sufferer from prickly heat on the face of the globe," Trotter said plaintively.

"I feel for you," North sympathized cheerily. "Shall we go?"

Trotter folded the letter he was writing to a girl who doubtless was convinced she was the Only One, stuck it in the pocket of his hand-tailored blouse, and stood up. He clicked his heels with exaggerated military precision and flourished a beautiful, if French, flat-handed salute. "We go, *mon colonel*," he said. "But if you knew what a babe I'm leaving to carry you to Zambo-Bango, or whatever it's called, you'd put me up for the Medal of Honor. And who are we after this time, or is it Top Secret?"

"We're after a man named George Lee," Hugh North said. "We want to take him under our protective wing before certain other characters make sure we don't."

ii

At the moment that Hugh North was telling Kenny Trotter where they were bound, a half-caste Malay, who went under many names but under the alias of George Lee more than most, was standing at El Chileno's crowded bar in Zamboanga.•

He did not look like a man who would evoke a top-priority message from the Pentagon. He wore a ragged pair of duck pants and a singlet, an ancient topee that was too big for him, and a pair of filthy sneakers. He was as thin as the knife at his belt, and his faintly slanted eyes might have belonged to a rabid fox, wary but dangerous.

He had come back to this steaming part of the world over a long trail, had George Lee, with an enforced stopover in the hands of the Chinese Communists. That had not been a pleasant time, and Lee intended to make up for it in a very big way when he cashed in.

Tomorrow, or the next day at the latest, George Lee would go to Sanga Sanga, and there he would meet somebody—poor fool—who would help him get some-

4

thing that would make the rest of his life a dream, a bloody rose-colored, sweet-scented dream.

"Can I buy you a drink, mister?"

Lee whipped up his head and peered from under the brim of the frayed sun helmet. It was a soldier who had spoken to him, and where he had been until quite recently, soldiers spelled cruelty, vicious brutality. But this was no Chinese Red; this was a kid American, a—what did they call themselves?—a G.I. over from Fort Winfield on Sanga Sanga, in town on a pass. He was not the one Lee had dreaded seeing. Of course he could have been sent by ——, but there was nothing to fear from this baby and George Lee had a thirst that had been long denied.

"Don't mind if you do." He smiled with a display of crooked, pitted teeth. "Man needs a drink in this weather."

The soldier smiled back, a soft smile that went with his amber-eyed fawn's face. *The Yanks are puttin' bloomin' fairies in uniform*, George Lee sneered silently and asked aloud, "You from Fort Winfield over on Sanga?"

The soldier signaled the bartender and nodded. "Uh-huh. You ever been over there, mister?"

"I may have," Lee said guardedly. "I been almost everywhere, one time or another." He weighed his caution, decided to ask his question. "Place with an old castle, ain't it?" he asked. "Overlookin' a lagoon, like?"

"That's it," the boy said. "The officers use the castle for their quarters. It's cooler there, I guess. Gee, I wish we had some place like that instead of the darned old quonsets."

5

Well, slap me on the wrist and call me Maisie. Lee raised his glass in a toasting motion and threw back his head to toss off the drink. The boy merely touched his glass to his lips, his jaguar's eyes on the other's scrawny throat.

"Paah! That went where it was needed," Lee gasped.

"Have another?" the soldier asked gently. "My dad always says a man can't walk on one leg."

Wait a minute, Lee's brain told him, *why is this guy buying? Could he be trying to get me drunk? Him, a snot-nosed kid, trying to make me talk, maybe? Hah!*

"You're mighty kind, sojer," the half-caste said, and the boy signaled the barkeep again. "You new out here?"

The G.I. nodded. "Just came out last month, and it's not at all what I thought it would be like, the tropics and everything." He sighed. "I've already put in for transfer, and, golly, I hope it goes through." His face clouded, a petulant child's. "It won't, though. Colonel Flood will never—"

"Flood?" Lee interrupted. "You mean Jack Flood, him that used to be a sergeant in Manila?"

The boy's eyes rounded. "Was the C.O. a *sergeant?*"

Lee hunched his thin shoulders. "Prob'ly another guy," he said. "I knew a bloke in Manila once named Flood and I heard he got to be an orficer, that's all. This feller was—"

He stopped short. The American soldier was staring past Lee, his eyes wide, his mouth ajar. *Danger!* Lee spun about, his hand going to the knife at his belt.

There were many men behind him, but none that paid any attention to the skinny derelict in the topee.

6

And that, to George Lee, meant that this guy had tricked him with the old look-out-behind-you stare.

He whirled back. The soldier's hand was snatched back in a swift blur, but the half-caste knew it had been poised over his glass of whisky. This brat was fixing his drink! This—this *baby* was one of Them!

The knife glimmered as it swept up in Lee's grip. It drove at the soldier's belly, but it never landed. The half-caste had a glimpse of the O of a pistol muzzle— *a lady's gun, no service pistol, that*—and then the slugs caught him in the chest, three of them, spat so closely together that the reports sounded like a single stuttering shot.

Lee doubled over, his knife clanging to the floor. His last thought before the blackness claimed him was, *It ain't fair—a blinkin' infant instead of the one I was lookin' out for.*

iii

"The pearls . . . all the pearls in the world . . . gotta get to Sanga Sanga."

Colonel North bent closer to the man on the hospital bed, straining to catch the faint mutter, his perspiration dripping on the sodden sheets. It was hot, unbearably hot. Even with so much depending on Lee living long enough to talk, despite the fact that Washington and Manila had waited for this man so long and here he was, close to everlasting silence on this earth, North was conscious of the heat. It struck at him through his tropical chino uniform; it sent the sweat trickling down his hard, lean body; it coated his tanned face with a mask of perspiration.

Zamboanga was living up to its reputation; the town must be the hottest place in the Sulu Archipelago this day, and the hospital ward where Lee lay dying must be the hottest spot in Zamboanga.

"Blue dog's belly," the man on the bed said, quite distinctly. "Flood . . . waited . . . doctor, where's doctor?"

"Right here," North said in a low voice. "But tell me about it first, Lee."

Miraculously, the prodding murmur reached the struggling consciousness of the wounded man. His heavy lids slid back jerkily, and his slanted eyes stared up at North. Comprehension flickered in the drained, yellow-gray face as Lee's eyes moved from North to the white-clad doctor at the foot of the bed. The half-caste looked back at the G-2 colonel.

"You get the little bastard that shot me?" he asked. "Who was he—who did They send?"

North spoke swiftly; there was not much time. "You tell me," he said. "It was in El Chileno's bar. Didn't you know him?"

The balding head moved weakly on the soaked pillow. "Never seen him before in my life. Tried to poison my drink, he did, and when I caught him he shot me. *They* sent him, damn 'em, after promisin' me . . ." His lips trap-jawed shut, and he closed his eyes, turned his face away.

The doctor, a diminutive Filipino, left the foot of the bed and moved to Lee's side, picked up a broomstick

8

wrist to check the pulse. His eyes met North's across the bed.

"This talking is bad," he said gravely. "It takes too much out of him."

"He's got to talk," North said evenly. "Do you think I'd be here if it wasn't something pretty big?"

The doctor considered. Yes, it had to be something pretty big to bring a jet plane streaking to the little port of Zamboanga, bringing a full colonel to the death-bed of a half-caste beachcomber shot in a bar brawl. Pearls, the man Lee had shouted, and something about a dog's blue belly; this case must not only be pretty big but very strange. Still, a doctor's first duty was to his patient.

"I'm sorry, Colonel, but you must wait until he's stronger."

"You know there's no time," North rapped back. "I've got to talk to him, Doctor, believe me!"

"Still, I must—"

"The blue dog's belly!" Lee cried wildly in an out-burst of delirium. "The Commies tried to make me tell but I never did!"

North was crouched over the wounded man again. "You can tell me, Lee," he said. "Or do you want Them to get away with this?"

The half-caste's hand came out and clutched North's arm weakly. "All right, all right," he gasped. "I was double-crossed so I'll do the same, huh? You—you go to Fort Winfield and you'll find—you'll find . . ." His breath failed and his skinny chest pumped agonizingly.

"You'd never guess in a million years," he choked.

"Thinks . . . safe. I'll tell you who—ahhhh, my God—doctor . . ."

The Filipino doctor was there, but he could do nothing now. As North repressed the wild urge to grab George Lee by the shoulders and *shake* those last words out of him, another spasm of pain wracked the half-caste. Lee writhed, arched, groaned, slumped back. His hoarse, rattling sigh told Hugh North that he was dead.

iv

Back at the flea-ridden oven that posed as a hotel, Kenny Trotter threw clothes into a kit bag with characteristic disorder and talked over his shoulder.

"I'm sure sorry your man died before he could talk, Colonel," he said, "but it does get us out of this hole, that's one thing." When the silence behind him persisted, he turned around slowly and asked, "Don't we? Leave Zamboanga, I mean?"

Hugh North nodded absently, deep in his thoughts. Reaching George Lee too late had been nobody's fault but the agent's who had lost Lee in Hong Kong, but the bitter pill he had just swallowed still tasted bad. He had been ordered to take the half-caste into protective custody and he had not; never mind the extenuating circumstances—Hugh North had never been a believer in alibis.

If he could have gotten to Lee before the man had walked into the bar at El Chileno's where the gunman waited, he could have kept Lee alive and Lee would have talked, finally. Oh yes, he would have talked, and not by means of brainwashing, either, such as the Commies had tried, futilely. Scopolamine, truth serum, was very valuable stuff, and in a place like Zamboanga there hardly would have been a headline-hunting lawyer spouting constitutional rights to prevent a nice, solid dose in George Lee's arm.

If only—but G-2 didn't operate on *ifs*.

"The aircraft is ready, *mon colonel*," Kenny said hopefully. "We can be in Manila in time for—"

"No soap, Lieutenant," North said. "We're going to Sanga Sanga, not Manila, and we're not leaving here until some information I've asked Washington for comes in by short wave."

"Sanga Sanga?" Trotter asked fearfully. "And where—"

"Sanga Sanga is an island in the Sulu Sea, twenty miles from here," North recited patiently, "and on Sanga Sanga is Fort Winfield. Winfield was an American outpost before Philippine independence. Now it's an American guided-missile base under the Philippines Military Assistance Act of 1946. It is commanded by a lieutenant colonel named Flood who once was a drill sergeant and who still chews out fresh young fly-boys who are not up on their military courtesy and discipline, no doubt. So, as the old lady said, mind your manners, bub."

He paused and added, "I told you that Zamboanga was the hottest place in the world. I now qualify that statement. There's one place that's hotter."

Kenny Trotter made a statement instead of asking a question. "Sanga Sanga," he said.

"Right." North grinned.

Trotter winced, but bravely. He might be a great admirer of cool, fan-swept places where long, tall drinks were served at tables where beautiful, soft-skinned young ladies sat across from him, but if his colonel's duties carried him to the gates of Hell, there would go Kenny Trotter with no more than a clamor of self-pity, meant only to maintain his pose. For while Trotter might act the flip insubordinate with North, in strict private (a fact that the official Army world never even slightly suspected) he was, actually, devoted to the point of worship to his superior, this tall, wide-shouldered colonel who roamed the world for the Criminal Investigation Division, United States Army.

"While we're waiting for the information," the young flier asked now, "can you fill me in on this case?"

North was training Lieutenant Trotter to follow in his footsteps, to take up where he left off on that dim and distant day of retirement, with a dress parade on some sunlit field with blaring bands and misty eyes. Hence he was careful to tell Kenny everything he should know about every case.

"It's like this, Junior," he said. "Before Pearl Harbor there was a Jap spy ring operating through the Philippines headed by a man named Hansen, Arnulf Hansen. That wasn't his real name, and he was about as much a Scandinavian as I am, but for purposes of identification, Hansen will do."

"And we're after this guy?" Kenny asked.

"No, if we know one thing sure about this case it's that Hansen got his back in '45," North said. "When he saw it was all over for the Nips, he took out of Manila aboard an old captured Chinese coaster, the *Kinshu Maru*, that had been the *Chu San*. The ship was sunk off Sanga Sanga—it was the last Jap convoy to try to slip through the Sulu Sea—and Hansen was killed. George Lee, Hansen's right-hand man, got away; he was picked up by a Jap destroyer, and when that vessel was torpedoed off the Chinese coast, Lee escaped again. He stayed in China, first as a red-hot Commie, and later, when he fell out with Big Brother Mao, as a guest in a prison at Shaowu. He was released, or escaped, not long ago and headed for here."

"Hansen's definitely dead?" Trotter asked.

"Take my word for it," North said firmly. "But we believe he left something behind that we want—the same thing Lee wanted and, obviously, the thing that whoever killed Lee had to keep him from getting."

"And what's that?"

"Well, for one thing, Hansen was carrying a fortune in pearls. It was his spy's payoff—better than currency and easier to carry than gold."

"Whoopee, pearls!" Trotter exulted. "All my life I've wanted to find the fabulous pearls that the sloe-eyed beauty was concealing somewhere about her lovely person."

"At ease," North groaned. "The pearls are minor-league stuff, actually. What we want to get our hands on is the microfilm Hansen valued more than the pearls. If we can find that film we'll know who Hansen's people really were and which ones might still be in the same racket."

"How do we know about the microfilm?" Trotter asked.

North shrugged. "The old story. Hansen had a woman in Manila. He promised to take her along when he left, but he crossed her up, left her behind. She should have been grateful that he didn't take her aboard the *Kinshu Maru*, perhaps, but she wasn't. When our people saved her from being torn apart as a collaborator she paid Hansen back by spilling everything she knew. It wasn't much aside from mention of that microfilm. She never saw it, but she knew Hansen photographed everything important that passed through his hands; that film contained the names of all his top paid traitors. As a blackmail instrument, it's probably worth more than the pearls. George Lee apparently thought so. And so did whoever killed him to keep George Lee from getting the film."

"Anything new on the killer, Colonel?" Trotter asked.

The G-2 colonel shook his head. "Not a thing," he said. "The fellow just vanished. All we know is that he was a baby-faced young man in an American uniform and the shoulder patch that fits the Fort Winfield guided-missile battalion. Everybody who saw him agrees that he looked like a mamma's boy." He grimaced. "Some mamma's boy, he and his little .28-caliber doll and his poison playthings."

Trotter's eyebrows went up a notch. "Poison?" he asked.

"Oh yes, he tried to poison Lee before he shot him. Quieter, you know, and he could have been gone before Lee fell over. Lee caught him dropping the stuff in his drink, and the kid had to use his gun. Not that it mattered much; everybody ducked, and when they came out he was gone."

"He tried to poison Lee, eh?" the pilot marveled. "It couldn't have been just an unlucky bar brawl, then."

"He tried to poison Lee, all right. Seems that after the shooting, in all the excitement, a barfly swooped down on those two drinks that were still on the bar, Lee's and the gunman's. They found the barfly stiff in an alley a couple of hours later. He had enough poison in him to kill a *carabao*. So that must mean—"

He stopped as a knock sounded at the door.

"That'll be my information," he nodded and went to the door, opened it to take a sheaf of papers from the sergeant of the Philippine constabulary who offered them with a salute.

"Thank you, Sergeant, and thank your C.O.," North said, returned the salute, and turned back into the room. Kenny Trotter reached for the code book. From the thickness of that sheaf of papers, Colonel North was going to find out all about a hell of a lot of people.

v

It was late that night when Hugh North finished decoding and digesting the voluminous report he had called for from top headquarters in the Pentagon. Outside, Zamboanga was quiet except for an occasional whoop from the direction of El Chileno's, where a particularly seamy life carried on, George Lee's murder forgotten. Moths swooped and fluttered about the drop light that hung down over the cluttered table where North sat; occasionally a bold rat scuttled across the floor; giant roaches traversed the walls in zigzag rushes.

Colonel North laid down his pen, pushed back his chair, and stretched with a yawn. Kenny Trotter, drooping across from the colonel, straightened and blinked the sleep aside.

"All set?" the lieutenant asked. "Do we take off now or do we spend another night in this firetrap?"

"I'm afraid we stay," North replied. "It'd be nice to drop in on Fort Winfield unannounced, but it's a missile base, remember, and surprise visits to missile bases aren't too healthy, ever. Besides, the field on Sanga Sanga is going to take some tight flying—it's a minimum for jets—and I don't relish your trying it in the dark. So we'll wait over until tomorrow—later today, rather—before we head for Sanga Sanga. Anyway, I want to make a last-minute check with the constabulary to see if they've possibly got something new on Lee's killer."

Trotter eyed the mass of papers in front of North. "And what did you get out of that bale of stuff, Colonel?" he asked.

North lit a cigarette, studying his scribbled notes. "What I wanted was some possible connection between the garrison at Fort Winfield and Hansen's old spy ring," he told his aide. "Somebody knew Lee was coming to Zamboanga and had a one-man reception committee waiting. That could mean that Lee himself sent word he was on his way; pretty trusting for a man like Lee, but still possible. The killer wore an Army uniform, something not easily come by except as issue, not in this part of the world. *Ergo,* the killer came from Fort Winfield. The tie with Sanga Sanga is definitely there."

He leaned forward to make a check mark, leaned back again. "Okay, we either have the killer operating on his own or being hired by somebody to dispose of George Lee. This boy was described as a baby-face. At the most he could be, how old—twenty-five? Twenty-five from—let's see—hmm—that would make him about eleven years old when Arnulf Hansen was killed, less than that when Hansen was doing his dirty work. A little young to be mixed up in a spy ring, I'd say. So we cross off the idea of the killer being on his own."

"Maybe it was just a bar fight," Kenny suggested. "Maybe it just happened that Lee and this guy . . ." He stopped as the stern eye of Hugh North was fixed upon him. "I forgot the poison, massa," he said meekly. "Excuse it, please."

"So we have the killer, X, working for somebody. Somebody at Sanga Sanga. Another enlisted man? Not likely; these records show that of the three hundred and eight enlisted men and noncoms at the missile base —it's a bobtailed battalion—only fourteen are old-timers; the rest are draftees, mostly youngsters like X. Of the fourteen who are old enough to possibly have known Hansen, only three were in this part of the world when Hansen was operating. Theoretically, these three are suspects. Here they are." He consulted a list.

"Private James Mulcahey, old Third Cavalryman, been up to top soldier and down again a dozen times, past retirement age but no idea of quitting the service, now permanent latrine orderly. Doesn't sound like our man, but you never can tell."

"Latrine orderlies are not poison killers," Trotter said firmly. "They get their men with ice water in the hot showers." He mopped his brow and sighed, "Gad, hot showers!"

"Numbers Two and Three are Tech Sergeant Norman Butler and Tech Sergeant Austin Hewett—damn these new specialist ratings, anyway. Both were with Wainwright at Corregidor, both survived the Death March. Hard to imagine a Hansen man having to go through that. I'd say mark 'em off."

"I'd say so, too," said Kenny Trotter.

"Now we come to the officers," the shadow-eyed colonel said after a drag on his cigarette. "And we find something very interesting." He picked up a sheet of paper and deciphered his own notes, no mean feat. "The four senior officers at Fort Winfield are field-commissioned men. They were all noncoms for years before the war. They served together in various Philippine posts. Each one had the opportunity to sell information to Hansen. None of them was trapped at Corregidor or went on the Death March."

He lowered the paper and pulled hard at his cigarette. "Any one of them, Lieutenant, is a firm, fully packed suspect for us. An officer at Fort Winfield could offer the most inducements to a murder-minded man—in fact, he would be most likely to know he had

18

a killer in the battalion, willing to do murder for a price."

"But an officer could also masquerade as an enlisted man and—damn it, there's the baby-face. These guys must be too old to still have a baby-face if they ever owned one," Trotter said.

"And a senior officer could hardly come over from Sanga Sanga to knock off Lee without being missed at the fort," North added. "An enlisted man could—he could even be detailed to come over. You see, if the poison business had worked, Lee could never have talked as much as he did. The crowd in El Chileno's wouldn't have had as much description of X as they did. If he hadn't had to shoot, X very possibly could have made it back to Sanga Sanga with nobody but his employer the wiser. A bum like Lee could collapse, die, and be buried with no more thought put to it than that bad liquor had caught up with him at last."

He looked down at the paper again, his mouth tightening. "But the poison didn't work, X had to shoot, and so now we have five suspects, each an officer in the United States Army."

He tolled them off.

"Flood, John Joseph, lieutenant colonel, commanding officer of the battalion.

"Macy, Hilton Roger, major, adjutant.

"O'Hare, Benjamin Quentin, captain, commanding A Company.

"Keene, Patrick Arnold, captain, commanding B Company.

"Rickerson, Arthur En-Em-Eye, first lieutenant,

commanding C Company, replacing Coulson, Forrest Jackson, captain, recently deceased."

He tossed the paper aside and reached for the ash tray to tap his cigarette. "The other three junior lieutenants are in the clear as far as possible implication in Hansen's spy ring is concerned," he told Kenny. "But as things look now, one of those five senior officers was a traitor, if he isn't still."

He paused, and his voice was grim when he said, "And God have mercy on him when I get the proof—he'll need it."

Chapter Two

●—■—●—■—●—■—●—■—●—■—●—■—●—■—●—■—●—■—●—■—●—■—●—■—●—■—●—■—●

i

SANGA SANGA was a crescent-shaped island humped out of the Sulu Sea almost perpendicularly, its steep rises pointing to a mountain peak down from which foamed a torrent that was clearly visible as Trotter brought the jet in from Zamboanga. As the details emerged from the dot in the water, Hugh North told his pilot to cut his speed and make a circle of the island.

"But get your recognition first," he counseled Kenny. "I've radioed them to expect us, but guided-missile bases are notoriously touchy about unidentified aircraft buzzing around."

Kenny nodded, and flipped open his transmitter. "Dog-Twelve-Hero," he announced, via his throat mike. "Dog-Twelve-Hero to Sanga Sanga. Approaching at four thousand. Over."

There was the rasping crackle of static, and then the blaring voice of Fort Winfield in the earphones. "Roger, Dog-Twelve-Hero. Use east-west runway.

Stay in aircraft until cleared by Oh-Dee. Repeat. Stay in aircraft until cleared by Oh-Dee. Over."

Kenny glanced at Hugh North, and the colonel nodded.

"Roger," the pilot said. "Request permission to circle island two times prior to landing. Over."

A longer stretch of static this time, and then the words, "Affirmative. Over."

"Roger and out," Kenny said, and broke off transmission contact. He brought the jet lower and swept over the island of Sanga Sanga while North peered from the cramped cockpit.

The island was a pretty spot from above, with the jungle coming down to sheer cliffs that fell off to the water's edge except for one sandy beach near the mouth of the foaming stream. About the only level places on Sanga Sanga were the landing strip, hacked out of volcanic rock, and a small parade ground. These stood out clearly; the other buildings of the installation were half or wholly hidden by the jungle, except for one great pile of masonry that perched on a promontory overlooking a sizable lagoon next to the beach.

A few of the poised missiles were visible from the air, but most were hidden by the palms, banyans and other tropical trees that choked the island. Not far from the castle and on a bay bordered by the sand beach was a small-boat dock and a modest seaplane ramp. Fort Winfield on Sanga Sanga was quite clearly a minor installation, one of the few remaining Army frontier outposts in this atomic age.

"Okay, take her in," North told Kenny, and Trotter flipped the jet over on a wing, screamed down onto the runway, flapped, touched and braked with gentle excellence. The pilot cut the thunderous engine as a jeep detached itself from the shadow of the one hangar across the field and raced toward them.

"What's the old tower?" Trotter asked as they awaited the officer of the day's arrival.

"The original Fort Winfield," North explained. "It belonged to the Spanish before Dewey took Manila." He forestalled Trotter's delighted comment. "No, I was not in that operation. About the castle, I understand it's used as officers' quarters now. And here comes our friend, the O.D., to let us out."

The two men alighted from the plane as a tall, powerfully built officer wearing captain's bars at his collar and a forty-five at his hip, leggings encasing his shins, a helmet liner on his head, left the jeep and walked toward them. The captain's hand came up in a salute.

"Colonel North?" the O.D. asked, no welcoming smile on his tanned, middle-aged face. "I'm Pat Keene, sir, O.D."

Hugh North returned the salute and thrust out his hand to meet a hard-muscled grip. "Sorry to bother you fellows, Captain Keene," he said. He squinted up at the fierce sun and added, "I should think you boys would wear tropical pith helmets instead of liners."

"We would," Keene said, the bitterness unconcealed, "but Colonel Flood says no."

North made a note of the venom in Keene's voice; everything was not palsy-walsy among the old-soldiers-turned-officers on Sanga Sanga, then; this was no closed corporation, and that was all to the good for his purposes. While he introduced Trotter to the officer of the day, the colonel kept his eyes on Keene. The captain's cheeks were deeply lined; the corners of his mouth were downdrawn; his eyes were noncommittal as they returned to North.

"I'm wondering if I know your Colonel Flood," North put out as a feeler. "Of course the name's not too uncommon, but I think I've known a man named Flood somewhere in the service."

"It's Jack Flood," Pat Keene explained. "We were noncoms together, both staffs in the Philippines in the old days. During the war I served under Jack—he made major almost right away—until I got my own commission. Later, when Flood got this wonderful post, he pulled strings to get me out here." The captain's mouth twisted viciously for a moment, and then he spat, "My pal!"

He caught himself immediately. "Put that down to the heat, Colonel," he said swiftly. "Colonel Flood's okay. We all pop off once in a while in this heat. Even the wives—"

"Wives!" North exploded. "Don't tell me there are women on this post!"

Keene nodded. "There shouldn't be, but there are. Mrs. Flood, Mrs. Coulson, Mrs. O'Hare and Mrs. Rickerson. They live in the castle—that's the original old fort over there on the lagoon. But let's get out of this sun."

"Can I take my aircraft in, Captain?" Kenny asked.

"Sure, go ahead," Keene nodded. "I suppose I'm expected to go through it with a fine-tooth comb—Jack's scared of spies with atom bombs—but go ahead, Lieutenant, take her in. Then come on up to the officers'

24

club for a drink—it's in the castle; anybody'll show you."

North got his attaché case out of the plane and joined Keene in the jeep. They rocketed across the field as, behind them, Kenny fired his engine again and began taxiing toward the apron. North looked about him, the rattle and jounce of the little quarter-ton discouraging conversation with the officer of the day, Keene.

As a guided-missile base, Fort Winfield had spread out from the original installation it had been. Bordering the landing strip at one side and set back in the jungle shade were quonset-hut barracks big enough to hold the bobtail battalion. There was also a palm-thatched headquarters building, a radio shack, a guardhouse, a station hospital, both close to the headquarters, warehouses, a powerhouse, an ice plant and an ammo dump. At one end of the parade ground the Stars and Stripes drooped dispiritedly from its flagpole.

Hugh looked beyond the postwar installation buildings toward the great heap of stone that reared its bulk on the point over the lagoon, outlining its cruel splendor against the brazen sky. The castle was of yellow-brown stone, Spanish in design, complete with battlements and watchtower. To North, the American flag that flew at the top of the tower was incongruous; a Jolly Roger would have been more in keeping.

The jeep drew up in front of the headquarters building with a skirl of marl and coral sand, and the perspiration-soaked pair alighted.

"Colonel Flood's not here right now," Captain Keene said. "Asked you to wait."

North took the announcement without a change of expression, no matter what he might have felt. The C.O. of Fort Winfield must know that this visit was no social call, not with the whole fort restricted until he, North, lifted the restriction. And yet this Colonel Flood, a lieutènant colonel with a field commission, asked full Colonel Hugh North of G-2 to wait.

So you wait, North told himself wryly, and pulled a pack òf cigarettes from his pocket, eyed them dismally; during the short jeep trip across the field the pack had been thoroughly soaked with sweat.

"Have one of mine," Pat Keene said, and passed over his moistureproof case as they walked into the C.O.'s office. Here fans whirled in two corners of the room, but outside of moving the sticky air sluggishly they seemed to be goldbricking; this heat was so humid, it sludged about like scummy water.

As North used his handkerchief on his streaming face, Keene chuckled mirthlessly. "Welcome to Sanga Sanga, Colonel," the O.D. said. "The glamorous Sulu Sea paradise. With the men restricted by your radio message, the place is really bad-tempered—I hope you can at least let the men go swimming before we have a supreme foul-up here."

"As soon as possible," North promised. "Were the men who were on pass in Zamboanga two days ago confined to quarters?"

"There wasn't anybody over there that day," Keene said. "Somebody in A Company goofed a test alert four days ago, and Colonel Flood canceled all furloughs and passes for a week. Nobody was off Sanga Sanga that day."

North took the news calmly. This development was to be expected; the man who killed George Lee would hardly have been a soldier on official pass.

"In that case," he said, "the restriction probably can be lifted as soon as I talk to the C.O." He mopped his face again and asked Keene, "How long have you been out here, Captain?" (No need to let anybody know about those records he had pored over in Zamboanga.)

"Too long," Keene grunted. "More than six years, all told."

"As long as that?" North murmured. "No request for transfer to someplace cooler?"

Keene snorted. "There's no such thing as a transfer out of Fort Winfield, Colonel. That sounds like a recruit's gripe, I know, but it's true. Flood seems to like it here, and he wants us with him, all his old pals." The word "pals" dripped sarcasm. "So when we put in for transfer it goes through channels with his first endorsement, *Not Approved*—if it goes through channels at all and not into the first sergeant's file, the wastebasket."

"How about the inspector general?" North asked.

"Look, Colonel," Keene said recklessly, "this is Sanga Sanga, not Fort Myer, right next to the Pentagon. The I.G. never gets out here, and even if he did—well, let's face it; most of us are overage in rank—we'd either be retired out or go back to master sergeant in grade if we moved someplace else." He barked a laugh. "So we gripe and stay in this Old Soldiers' Home—this Jack Flood Refuge for Mustang Officers."

There was a brief silence, and then North asked another checking-up question. "How many field-commissioned old pro's are there here, Captain?"

"There's Major Macy, the adjutant, and the company commanders, me, Bottles O'Hare and Art Rickerson, besides Flood. Rick's a first John. He took over Creepy Coulson's company when Creepy did the commit last month."

North had read only that Captain Lester Scott Coulson had shot himself the previous month while temporarily deranged. Perhaps there was something more to be learned here.

"Did the commit?" he asked Keene.

"Yeah—you know—shot himself. The heat."

If North thought it was an extremely offhand way to pass over the suicide of a brother officer, he let it pass. He could come back to it later, and meanwhile there were those women. They were something new to North; no part of his report from Washington had mentioned wives.

"How many ladies are there on the post, did you say?" he asked.

"Four. Estelle Flood, Manuela Rickerson, Annie O'Hare and Janice Coulson, Creepy's widow. She's leaving pretty soon, I guess." He shot a sudden look at North. "Are you here about old Creepy's suicide, Colonel? Somebody ought to chew Flood out about that. Jeez, Jack knew Creepy was—" He buttoned his mouth abruptly.

Hugh North waited and then said, "No, I'm not here about Captain Coulson, but I'm interested. When did he shoot himself?"

"About five weeks ago. I thought you knew."

28

Keene's mouth twisted in a cheerless smile. "Uh-huh, old Creepy used to laugh about Killer Castle, and you see what happened to him."

"Killer Castle?"

Keene hunched his wide shoulders. "That's the name the old fort got a long time back. When the Spaniards owned this joint, the commandant went nuts from the heat or something and murdered half the garrison before they knocked him off. Since then there's been a lot of peacetime killings here—spicks, Americans, the Japs when they occupied this island. The natives say the place is damned." He looked through the window at the tower that thrust its bulk over the lagoon. "I'll go along with that."

He moved his somber eyes back to North.

"Blame it on the heat if you want to, Colonel," he said, "but there's something—something *evil* about this place, the castle, the whole damned island. It got Coulson, no matter what Flood put on the report. It'll get a lot of good men before it's through. Heat and bugs and snakes and fever and too much booze and not enough women—or too many, when they all start bitching at once—and everybody hating everybody else's guts, that's Sanga Sanga."

He raised a lean and faintly trembling hand to wipe at the sweat on his forehead.

"You sure picked one fine little hellhole when you decided to come to Sanga Sanga, Colonel," he said.

ii

North kept his easy smile as he puffed at his cigarette, tapped the ash in a tray on the desk. This must be quite a place, this Sanga Sanga, when it could make a hard-boiled ex-sergeant like Pat Keene get this spooked. Or was Keene hagridden by inner torments that never let up on him?

"You know how it is, Captain," he said negligently. "You go where you're sent in this man's Army and, at the risk of sounding like Jack Armstrong, the All-American boy, you try to do your job, no matter where. And speaking of doing your job, where is Colonel Flood, anyway?"

Keene said, after a pause, "I suppose he's taking his siesta, sir."

"Taking his *what?*"

The middle-aged captain gave up whatever effort he had made to smooth over the situation. "This is a fouled-up post, Colonel," he said bluntly, "and that goes for everybody in it, including the C.O. Yeah, Flood takes a nap every damned day, and nobody had better disturb him when he's sacked in, either."

North's mouth was a thin line. "Where's his quarters, Keene?" he snapped. "We'll see if that *don't disturb* sign goes for me."

Keene began to backwater. "Hell, I didn't mean to pop off about Jack," he said. "I guess he runs an all-right outfit here, everything considered. It's just this lousy heat and—"

"I'd say the heat is about worn out as an excuse for everything, Captain," North crackled. "I've been at other tough posts, and the troops there were soldiering and their officers were, too—not sacking in while I wore out the seat of my breeches waiting on their convenience. Do you take me to Colonel Flood or do I find him myself?"

"Oh, I'll take you, Colonel," Keene said, "but—"

"Never mind the buts, Captain Keene! I want to see your C.O. Right now!"

Keene stiffened under North's whiplash voice. He braced himself into the position of attention and snapped, "Yessir." He wheeled and stalked out of the headquarters office, North at his heels, seething. They crossed the parade ground, North conscious of the many watching eyes. The colonel reminded himself that word traveled fast on any Army post; at Fort Winfield on Sanga Sanga, with the lack of much else to do to pass the time, the hot-poop grapevine must be a lulu. And was the baby-face who had killed George Lee watching him? Would he make a break for it?

Keene and North came to an arched gate which once had been reached by a drawbridge. The entrance to the great building was heavily ornamented with elaborate carvings, the lions and towers of Castile still discernible in the keystone of the yawning portal. The two men crossed a stone-paved courtyard that once had been a drill square and followed a shaded gallery to a flight of worn stone steps.

"We'll try the clubroom first," Keene said. "Flood might be there by now."

And he better hadn't be shooting a game of pool!

North told himself furiously and kept his frigid silence as he followed Keene into the wide, white-walled room decked with faded guidons and war trophies. Three officers seated in a tight-knit circle of wicker chairs turned their faces toward North and, at the glint of the silver eagles on Hugh's open collar, sprang to their feet.

"Where's the colonel?" Keene asked brusquely.

The biggest of the officers, a thick, red-faced man, put a sneer in his answer. "Where else but in his bood-war?" he asked. His pink eyes looked at North, and he introduced himself. "O'Hare's the name, Colonel."

The man's breath reached North's nose and told him why Captain Benjamin Quentin O'Hare bore the nick-name "Bottles." Hugh managed an answering smile; could a man be blamed too much for lapping it up off duty at a post like this?

"Hugh North," he said briefly in the absence of any evidence of a general introduction by Keene.

"Not the famush—famous Colonel North of G-2!" O'Hare exclaimed. He turned, and his voice blared. "Hey, fellers, look who's here! Colonel North himself, come to Sanga Sanga to find out how Flood can be such a bastard, I bet!"

"At ease, Bottles." A short, well-groomed major stepped forward. "Don't mind him, Colonel," he said. "That's last night's Tom Collins talking. I'm Macy, adjutant." Like Keene, O'Hare and the other officer in the room, Major Macy was in his forties, at least, and there was Old Army stamped on his face with the indelibility visible to another Old Army man, Hugh North.

"This is Lieutenant Rickerson," Macy said, with a hand wave at a tall, Lincolnesque officer. "We heard you were coming, of course, Bottles' little act notwithstanding. Care for a drink, Colonel?"

"I want to see Colonel Flood immediately," North told the adjutant crisply. "I understand he's taking his siesta, but I've got to see him now."

Macy darted a reproachful glance at the scowling Keene and shook his head. "It's not really a siesta, Colonel," he said. "It's malaria."

"Malaria!" O'Hare grunted and followed it with a blunt stable sergeant's word.

Macy whirled toward Bottles, his face red beneath its tan. "By God, if I were you I'd give Jack a little loyalty for all he's done for you, O'Hare," he rasped. "You and your—"

"Hold it, Mace," boomed a voice from the doorway, and Hugh North turned to meet the commanding officer of Fort Winfield on Sanga Sanga.

iii

Lieutenant Colonel Jack Flood was a bull of a man, his powerful body shaped like a huge capital V, his small round head crowned by close-cropped, sun-bleached bristles, set on a red, massive neck that went with the undershot jaw, the broken nose, the scar that drew a crooked line across his left cheek down to the corner of the hard mouth.

His eyes were small and openly hostile as he spoke to North.

"Colonel North? What's the idea of puttin' a goddam restriction on my post?" was his opening salvo. "What's G-2 messin' around with now?"

Hugh North held hard to the reins of his temper. "I think we'd better talk about that in your office, Colonel," he said quietly.

Flood scowled and cast his eyes about the clubroom. "Okay," he said grudgingly. "I guess you're right—too many big ears listenin' here. Be all over hell in five minutes if you tried to keep it private around this place." His glare fastened on O'Hare. "Drunk again, hey, Bottles?" he asked contemptuously. "Boy, you're really buckin' for trouble, aren't you?"

O'Hare glared back at his C.O., his contempt as heavy as Flood's. "You try makin' trouble for me, Jack," he gutturaled, "and we'll see who hurts the worst before it's over."

"As you were!" Major Macy snapped.

There was a tense, taut moment, broken by the arrival of Kenny Trotter in the doorway, followed by an enlisted man who carried North's bag and Kenny's luggage. North seized on the pilot's arrival as a chance to still the gathering storm.

"Can you assign quarters for my pilot and me, Colonel?" he asked Flood. "This is Lieutenant Trotter, gentlemen, my pilot."

"Not an Air Force guy," Lieutenant Rickerson groaned.

Kenny Trotter took in the situation with a practiced eye. "When you say that, smile!" He laughed and brought an answering chuckle from O'Hare, Macy

34

and Rickerson. Flood's scowl subsided, and he turned to toss an order at Macy.

"See that the colonel and his pilot are fixed up," he told the adjutant. "Make 'em comfortable—or as comfortable as you can in this tomb. This way, Colonel North."

Hugh followed Jack Flood out of the clubroom, fairly *feeling* the hate directed at the C.O. burning the small of his back. He had been on Army posts where the morale was low, where the C.O. was at odds with his officers, but never had he hit a place where the enmity was so open, where all the wraps were off.

"You goin' to be with us long?" Flood asked, with a glance at the attaché case in North's hand.

"It depends," Hugh said mechanically. "You never know in this business."

Flood grunted again (he was a great one for that, Hugh had already learned) and walked up on the porch of the headquarters building, stood aside to let North enter. In the office North had quitted so recently, Flood waved a meaty hand toward a chair, while he lumbered behind his desk and threw himself down in his creaking swivel chair, his head framed by the window behind him.

"Now," he said, "what can I do for you?"

Hugh North did not raise his voice, but his words flicked out across the desk with a bullwhip's sting.

"First," he said, "you can get it through your head that my department doesn't send me out sight-seeing, so I must be here for a fairly important reason. Next, that goddam restriction you mentioned back there wasn't put on this post for kicks. Third, when I'm called on by a superior officer I usually get off my butt and meet him."

"I didn't know what time—"

"I'm speaking, Colonel Flood! I don't give a damn about having to wait in this heat while you finished your siesta except during that time the man I'm after could be getting away."

Flood was silhouetted against the window, but North could see his saturnine features force themselves into a wry grimace.

"Okay, so I owe you an apology," the big man said. "My radio shack got the message about you comin' okay, but the operator said static was so rough he couldn't make out your arrival time. I was at the field at dawn, and I would've been there when you landed except the old malaria hit me hard and I had to lay down. I told Keene to get word to me on the double when your aircraft called in, but he didn't. He wouldn't. He'd rather make it look bad for me."

North considered. *It could be as Flood says; Keene acts as though he'd like getting Flood in bad with me, right at the start. O'Hare may have put a name to the malaria excuse, but Macy called it gin talking. And this isn't finding out who killed George Lee, anyway.*

"All right, I'll buy that," North said quietly. "Let's forget it. Now, I've got a description of a man who might be one of yours. He was mixed up in a shooting at El Chileno's in Zamboanga."

Flood cursed. "That goddam town," he said. "I'd put it off limits if it wasn't the only place around here where a soldier can let off steam to keep himself from goin' nuts. How bad is this shootin', Colonel?"

"Pretty bad. The other man died. He was a half-caste Malay named George Lee."

He gave Lee's name offhandedly, and it did not seem that he was watching Flood particularly closely when he said it, but he caught the reaction in the C.O.'s little eyes. What was it? Fear? Hate? Surprise? Whatever it was, Jack Flood knew George Lee. *Check!*

"Ever hear of him?" he asked idly, into the silence.

Flood hunched thick shoulders. "Who, Lee? Hell, I've met a hundred Lees, I guess, in thirty-three years in this man's Army."

"This one was a half-caste Malay."

"Then I didn't know him," Flood lied. "I make it my business not to know any gooks at all. I can't stand 'em. They say they're our allies, but to me they all stink—why, the guy that used to be top man on this island turned out to be a goddam traitor and a spy. And Rick had to marry his daughter!"

"You mean Esteban Ortega, the one who owned the copra plantation on the other side of Sanga Sanga?"

Flood's eyes were wary as he nodded. "You know a lot about this place, huh?" he asked. "You been here before?"

"No, I just studied up on it when I got this case," North explained.

Flood used thick fingers to run through his bristly hair. "I don't get it," he complained. "A gook gets knocked off in a bar fight and G-2 sends a colonel out on it. What gives?"

Again, North weighed his answer. If Flood was lying about knowing Lee, did that mean he was number-one suspect in this case? Possibly. So how best to

work it—play it cozy or do the open-faced act, making
Flood think that he, North, was completely conned?
Better try the cloak-and-dagger gambit; Flood would
be expecting something like that, and anything else
might make him suspicious.

"Let's say G-2 has its reasons," he said mysteriously.
"About the man who killed Lee, here's a description:
five-five or six, slight build, young features—a real
baby-face—funny eyes, like a cat's. Curly blond or
reddish hair, and he speaks with almost a lisp."

A malicious grin overspread Flood's battered face.
"Jee-zuss!" he exclaimed. "That sounds like that pansy,
Laval, Paul Laval! I'll admit, Colonel, I don't know
the names of half a dozen of these young recruits in
the battalion, but I know that jerk by the description.
Laval—why, that fairy wouldn't have the guts to knock
a sick whore off a toilet seat. Paul Laval shootin'
George Lee—that's a laugh!"

"George Lee didn't laugh much," North said dryly.
"Matter of fact, when I saw him, Lee wasn't laughing
about anything."

"You talked to him—you talked with Lee?" Flood
asked, suddenly sobered.

"A little." North nodded.

"What did he say—did he tell you about Laval or—
or anything else?" the big onetime sergeant asked.

"He talked a little. Let's get this man Laval in here,
and let me ask him a couple of questions."

As he spoke, North heard the rattle of rifles, the
shuffle of feet, the murmur of men, outside the headquarters building on the parade ground. He swung his
head toward the window in time to see Captain Keene's

helmet, go past the screened opening in the rapidly falling dusk.

"Guard mount," Flood supplied. He called through the connecting door to an outside office. "Hey, Sergeant, ask Captain Keene to step in a minute."

He looked back at North, his grin returned. "If you want to talk to Laval, I'll have Keene bring him in—he's in Keene's company," he said. "But much as I'd like to see that little jerk shanghaied out of here for good, it couldn't have been him, Colonel. Y'see, I had the whole battalion—"

Thwuccckkkk!

There was the solid smack of a bullet hitting the wall behind North, inches from his head. A split second later came the flat crack of a carbine.

iv

North instinctively slid sideways out of his chair. His hand automatically streaked to his thigh, then halted. He was not carrying a gun; he had not thought he would need one so soon. Which proved, he told himself grimly, that even an old hand at this game could be stupidly complacent at times.

Flood was hurtling toward the window where a neat O showed in the screen.

"Grab that man, Keene!" he roared. "Grab that snipin' sonofabitch!"

From outside there came an excited gabble, and above the uproar Keene shouted, "Cagnieri, drop that piece! Drop it, I tell you!"

North was at Flood's heels as the commanding officer of Fort Winfield dashed out of the office. Rounding a corner, they came upon a knot of soldiers struggling with a screaming, cursing, sobbing private.

"Lemme go!" the pinioned man screeched. "I'll get the—"

As North opened his mouth to yell "*Hold it!*" Flood reached the kicking, wrestling soldier, drew back a hamlike fist, and smashed it into the private's face. The soldier sagged in the grip of those who struggled with him, knocked out.

Flood turned to Captain Keene, his jaw jutting. "What's the idea?" he bellowed. "You tell that man to shoot me in the back of the head, maybe?"

Keene's reply blared as loudly as his C.O.'s accusation. "Too bad the poor sonofabitch didn't connect! I told you he was ready for the psycho ward, but you said he was goldbricking; you told me to drill the guy, rub his nose in it. I wouldn't blame him for takin' a pot shot at you, but he didn't. He just snapped off a round by accident at rifle inspection, and that made him flip his lid. He knew you'd do just what you're doin'—accuse him of trying to murder you."

North searched the parade ground until he found the shell that the carbine had ejected. He swiveled his eyes until he found the window through which the slug had crashed. He told himself it was a weird inspection arms that would send an accidentally fired round from where Cagnieri had stood through the window of Flood's office; by rights the bullet should have slanted skyward at a sharp angle.

Cagnieri might have been sent·off his rocker by the

heat, but he had meant that carbine bullet to hit Lieutenant Colonel Jack Flood.

Or Colonel Hugh North.

"Hey, you, Laval!" Flood was blaring. "You have anything to do with this?"

The G-2 colonel looked in the direction the C.O. was pointing. There, topped by a helmet liner that was part of the guard uniform, stood a small, slender young man whose face belonged on a timid schoolboy, not a killer. But the description fitted. Here was Baby-Face himself, Private Paul Laval.

The effeminate youth was staring at Flood, his fawn's eyes filled with astonished alarm. The girl's lips trembled in a stutter before Laval could find his voice.

"N-n-no, sir," he managed. "I was just standing beside Vince—beside Private Cagnieri, sir—when all of a sudden he began to curse—oh, it was dreadful—and he picked up his gun and—"

"It's a carbine, dammit," Flood snapped. "Don't they even teach you recruits the difference between a rifle and a carbine and a gun?"

A titter swept over the crowd, wrenched from the other soldiers by the tension, and Laval flushed. "No sir," he stammered. "I mean, I guess it was a carbine—I mean . . ." His girlish voice trickled off into a confused silence.

"Argh, you mean!" Flood said heavily. He looked at North and grinned. "Here's your man, Colonel North," he said. "Here's the one G-2's lookin' for."

"But sir!" Laval squealed. "I didn't shoot the gun—Vince did!"

"Oh, we're not sayin' you took that pot shot at me," Flood jeered. "The colonel's got you pegged for somethin' worse than that." As Laval went pale, the C.O. turned his back deliberately and began roaring orders to take Cagnieri to the guardhouse.

Laval fixed his curious eyes on North. "What does he mean, sir?" he asked. "I didn't do it, I swear, Colonel. Ask anybody. I was just standing there beside Vince, when all of a sudden he—"

"I know," North said quietly. He reached out to take the carbine from Laval's nerveless grip. Not that it was necessary, perhaps, but guards' weapons carried a live clip and North wanted no second "accidental" snap-off. "I want to talk over something with you, soldier. Suppose we go into the headquarters building here."

As the other men divided their wide-eyed attention between Laval and the unconscious Cagnieri's removal, North led the trembling young soldier to Flood's office. There he passed his hands over Laval's shrinking form, found no hidden .28, and then put him in a chair. The carbine he put on the top of the desk, within easy reach, as he took the swivel chair.

"I—I don't know what this is all about, sir," the baby-faced boy quavered. "This—this searching me and —and—maybe I ought to have stopped Cagnieri, but I didn't know what he was goin' to do until—"

"Sure," North broke in. "Never mind that. Who got you to kill George Lee?"

Laval's fright crumpled into panic. Too swiftly, too completely. The average man, the *innocent* man, would not have understood the question enough to be scared by it; Laval had been expecting the accusation of Lee's murder; he had had his act ready.

"K-k-killed George Lee?" the private gasped. "Oh, goodness, I didn't—what do you mean, sir?"

Behind all this show, on the drill field and in this office, there was a solid confidence, possessed by the soldier and sensed by North. Laval might stutter and tremble, but actually he was convinced that he had nothing to fear from this C.I.D. colonel or anybody else. His basic self-confidence permitted him to do all this posing as a sissified soldier; a man who was afraid would never dare play the role.

North eyed his prisoner closely. Consummate actor Laval might be, but he was bolstered by something beyond his histrionic talents, something that gave him this supreme self-confidence. He was not drunk, obviously, and so . . .

"I know you didn't kill Lee on your own, Laval," North rapped out. "Somebody hired you to knock off Lee. Who was it, and what did you get for it, a charge of heroin?"

The boy's face stiffened with real shock at that, his eyes round and staring, his effeminate good looks twisted into a grotesque mask for one moment as his eyes scrambled about the room, the caged puma's. He returned to North, his voice roughening a fraction.

"I don't know what you're talkin' about," he said. "I didn't kill anybody. I never heard of George Lee." His eyes sought the doorway, and he added, "Ask Colonel Flood if I could have killed anybody."

The big commanding officer of Fort Winfield lounged into the office and leaned back against the doorframe, his arms crossed over his wide chest. "Don't ask me to alibi you, Laval," he grated. "Like I told the colonel, I'd like nothin' better than to get you out of here—you with your Sweet William talk and your tryin' to cozy up to my wife." He looked over at Hugh. "Stick him with it if you can, Colonel," he said. "I dunno how the little jerk could've done it, but if you say he did it's fine by me."

Colonel North drew a deep inward sigh. How long, he asked, would he have to put up with Flood's crudities before he could wind up this case and then have the pleasure of telling Lieutenant Colonel Jack Flood what a lousy excuse for a commanding officer he was? *But when I do*, he added, dismally, *he'll chalk it all up to the fact that I went to the Point and he didn't, so it's just a snob talking.*

"If you don't mind, Colonel Flood," he said aloud, an edge to his voice, "I'd rather talk to Laval alone."

Flood wanted to stay, to listen and sneer *(or scare this boy into silence?)*, but North's tone gave him no choice. He shrugged and moved out of the office, banging the door shut behind him. North waited a moment, picked up the carbine, crossed to the door and listened. There was the muted bustle of the main orderly room but no sound—nor too much of the lack of it—to indicate that anyone listened in the hallway outside. He recrossed the office to the window and pulled it down. Night had fallen, abruptly as it always did in the tropics, but it was still breathtakingly hot; the torpid temperature inside the room had already reached such a level that the few degrees added by the closed window made no difference.

44

North resumed his seat behind the desk, the carbine handy. "Okay, Laval," he said, "let's hear the whole story."

Laval had recaptured his baby-face role. "But sir"— he trembled—"there's nothing to tell—cross my heart."

"Come on," North said impatiently, "let's not waste time. The longer you play games with me, the longer it'll be till the next fix for you. And don't give me any stuff about you not being on it; it sticks out all over you. Who but a hophead would think he could ever get away with killing Lee."

Laval dropped the mamma's-boy part he had been playing so expertly. "You're crazy," he snarled.

"Look," North said, "be sensible and give. We know you killed Lee, and we can prove it. There were a dozen witnesses. There were your fingerprints on the glass you left on the bar, and have you forgotten that you were printed when you came in the service, if not before? Oh, we know you killed Lee—what we want to know is who hired you to do it."

He made these statements with the calm assurance of a man who had checked fingerprints, who had a small army of witnesses all ready to identify Paul Laval. Actually, he was giving the soldier what Kenny Trotter was fond of referring to as "the old nothing-ball pitch." There were no fingerprints; the derelict who had poisoned himself with the stolen drink had taken care of that. A hundred beachcombers and bar-flies had witnessed the killing, perhaps, but they had offered little beyond the fact that the killer had been a G.I. who looked like a child. Possibly they could be persuaded to identify Laval in a line-up, but not probably; the inborn hatred for police held by that tribe would more likely urge them to protect any and all evildoers.

As Laval remained silent, shaking his blond head, the oversized helmet liner wagging back and forth, North took a different slant. "Maybe you don't know, Laval, that the people who put you up to this are going to want you very dead now that you've done your job. You're a junkie, and your boss knows junkies can be made to talk. So whoever hired you probably has plans already to slip some poison in your drink or use a knife or a gun on you when you least expect it. As a matter of fact, how do you know Cagnieri's shot just now wasn't intended for you?"

Wrong stab; Laval's amber eyes gleamed triumphantly.

"That wop didn't aim at *me*," the pretty boy sneered. "About the rest of it, that's—"

"All right, then," North graveled, "we'll play this straight if you want it that way. Where's the cute little .28 you used on Lee? Where did you get it? How did you know Lee was out of prison?"

Whatever Laval had fed his veins was in full command now. He lounged back in his chair, insolently asprawl, a sneer on his face.

"Keep talkin'," he told North. "When you're through I'll let you in on a secret. The regular records, the morning report and all the rest, will show you I wasn't off Sanga Sanga when Lee was killed. If I wasn't off Sanga Sanga, how could I kill Lee in Zamboanga?"

"Ahhh," Hugh North breathed, "and how did you know Lee was killed in Zamboanga?"

For one fleeting second, anger streaked through Laval's eyes, fury at having let his high-riding confidence betray him into a slip. "You said so yourself," he growled.

"Try again," North said pleasantly. "I didn't mention Zamboanga—I was careful not to."

"Then I heard Lee was shot in Zamboanga. So somebody told me."

"A few minutes ago you said you never heard of George Lee."

"I could've said anything. I guess some of the guys were over in Zamboanga and they heard about the shooting and they told me. I got a bum memory."

"You sure have," North sympathized. "Otherwise you'd remember that Colonel Flood had canceled all passes and furloughs on account of that goof-off in A Company on the test alert. Nobody was off post, legally, when Lee was killed."

"So how could I have shot him?" Laval shrugged.

"So how could some of the guys have told you about it?" North asked with a twin shrug.

Laval's eyes suddenly went hot, blazing with a mad light that went eerily with that angelic face. He had a rage as unbalanced as the rest of him, and it took over now. "Look, Colonel Whatchaname," he rasped, "lay off me, willya? Get off my back before I get good and sore."

"You scare me to death," North taunted. "What're you going to do to me, junkie, poison my drink? You're not packing that .28 now, you know."

47

Laval's face twisted viciously. "You got nothin' on me, copper," he spat. "Not one goddam thing."

"I've got you as an addict, if nothing else," North said cheerfully, "and I can start from there. Ever try the cold-turkey cure, Laval? It's right rough, but a hard guy like you can probably stand it."

Laval cursed deeply. "You ain't scarin' me," he told North. "I got friends."

"Sure." The G-2 colonel nodded. "Only those friends won't hold still for you being around to talk, not if they can help it. If you're chewing up the sheets in a hospital, under withdrawal, anything you tell about them won't count—you'll be crazy with the sickness. But after you get well enough to have your confession count, look out, Laval, look out."

For the first time, the boy's eyes wavered and fell. "You're feedin' me a line," he muttered. "My friends wouldn't cross me."

"No? You don't know who you're dealing with, kid. You don't know what's at stake here. They probably told you this was a peanut-stand job so you wouldn't hold them up too bad for your pay-off. What was it, H or M?"

Laval's eyes were back at North's, narrowed now. "You say a gook bum was mixed up in somethin' big?" he asked.

"So big you'd never have touched it with a ten-foot pole if you'd known," North said, nodding. "The pearls alone are worth—they tell you about the pearls?"

"No—what pearls?" The words were out before Laval could trap them behind his thinned lips.

North gave a short laugh. "Boy, they didn't tell you *anything*, did they? They really played you for a jerk, Laval."

The choirboy mask was entirely gone now, and in its place was a weasel's snarl.

"What goes here?" Laval cried. "This job was supposed to be a—"

And that was the end of Paul Laval's story. At that instant, as Hugh North leaned forward over the desk, the window with a screen already holed by Cagnieri's carbine bullet shattered into a thousand fragments. Laval leaped from his chair, did three or four steps of a frantic jig, and then crumpled. His face was not pretty now; there was the red stain of a bullet hole under one staring eye.

Chapter Three

NORTH LEAPED to the side of the window, the carbine unlocked, and peered out into the night. Lights were bobbing about outside, scattered shouts mounted to pandemonium; the killer would hardly be tarrying for a second shot. The G-2 colonel whirled and ran from the office, twisted down the corridor and out the door to the parade ground.

The swiftly descended darkness was turned back into blazing day as some master control switched on the giant floodlights that ringed the base, and Hugh North saw a shifting tangle of men milling in confusion. Then, above the tumult, came the blatted summons of a bugle, blaring from the amplifiers. It was the alert, and North silently damned whoever had sounded it. Now every man at Fort Winfield could run—*had* to run—to his post among the guided missiles. No chance to pick a fleeing killer out of that stampede.

North turned to go back to Laval and slammed into Pat Keene, coming from the hospital, next door.

"You all right, Colonel?" the other officer gasped. "They said Cagnieri was gunning for you."

"Cagnieri?"

"Hell, yes! He went berserk in the hospital. Joe Denver took him out of the guardhouse and put him there. Said he was sick. Sick, huh! He beat up Joe and went out the window. Denver said he had a gun and he was yelling about how he was going to kill you. And he must have got somebody—did you hear that shot?"

"It was Laval," Hugh North said bleakly. "He's in Flood's office."

Keene's jaw dropped. "Laval, that sissy kid you were putting through the wringer? What'd Cagnieri do, miss you and get Laval?"

North's voice was weighted by self-blame; he should have questioned Laval somewhere where nobody could have gotten to the suspect, not in a Grand Central Terminal like the C.O.'s office. "Don't ask me," he told Keene. "About all I know is that as soon as I get close to anything on this case somebody gets shot and I'm back where I started. Better get a doctor for Laval, if you have one at this lovely place. Not that I think a doctor will do Laval any good."

"I'll get Joe." Keene nodded. "He's all right now— just knocked out for awhile. Cagnieri must have gone completely nuts. You stay in the office. Don't go wandering around with that wild man gunning for you." He went off at a gallop, his .45 flapping at his thigh.

North slowly, thoughtfully, retraced his steps to the C.O.'s office. As he crossed the threshold, Flood's hard voice greeted him.

"Did you really have to shoot the kid, Colonel?"

The big onetime sergeant straightened from his crouch beside Laval's body, the ursine face taut, the undershot jaw pushed forward more than ever, his little eyes burning with hostility. Flood looked down at the carbine in North's hand and then back at Laval.

"I suppose he made a break for it, huh?" he asked Hugh and added, with insulting emphasis, "*After* he confessed he killed Lee."

North's temper strained at its leash, subsided under the colonel's iron self-discipline. "He was about ready to admit he shot Lee," he said quietly, "but I didn't kill him—the shot came through that window. Keene tells me Cagnieri escaped, saying he was gunning for me. He could have aimed at me and hit Laval."

"Not Cagnieri," Flood said heavily. "That guy might be off his rocker, but he made Expert with the .45. If he'd been aimin' at you, he'd have got you, Colonel."

"That was no .45 that killed Laval," North said. "Maybe Cagnieri's not so good with a .28."

"A .28?" the C.O. cried. "You're sure? That's a woman's gun."

"I know. The same caliber that killed George Lee."

Flood swung his heavy face around to stare at Laval, then looked back at Hugh North. "But if Laval killed Lee, how did Cagnieri get . . ." He stopped.

"You tell me," North said with a sigh.

There was a rap on the doorframe, and Captain Keene entered, followed by an officer North had not met before. This man carried a doctor's bag, he wore the staff-and-serpent insigne of the Medical Corps on his open collar opposite the major's leaf, and his face marked him as a man of medicine. His iron-gray hair and clipped mustache, the heavy-rimmed glasses he wore, all seemed to label the major an M.D.

His smile was part of a professional bedside manner, too, as he stepped up to North with outstretched hand. "Joe Denver, Colonel," he said. "Post surgeon—and feeling the need of some medicine myself right now, in the shape of a good stiff drink. That was one hell of a wallop Cagnieri gave me."

He raised a hand to the side of his head, just under the edge of his cap, and winced. North saw an ugly bruised cut, stained by Merthiolate.

Before North could more than murmur a "Too bad," the surgeon turned to Laval and looked down at the dead man, his lips pursed. "So his troubles are over, eh?" he said briefly, and knelt to go through the motions of searching for the pulse and heartbeat that were not there. He arose and swung around to face Flood.

"Never knew what hit him," he announced. "And I suppose poor Cagnieri is in big trouble."

"Maybe he wouldn't be if you hadn't been so goddam chicken-hearted," Flood said harshly. "Why didn't you leave him in the guardhouse where he belonged?"

Denver's angry response was checked by a rueful twist of his lips. "I guess you're right, Jack," he said honestly, "but I still say Cagnieri needed medical treatment more than a guardhouse cell. I ought to have kept the guard with us, I admit, but I thought Cagnieri was cooled off then and . . ." He hunched his trim shoulders and said, "Okay, so I was wrong. All I hope is that your trigger-happy men don't shoot that sick boy on sight."

"Sick boy," Flood growled. "The guy tries to kill me and Pat says, oh no, it was an accident. Now that he gets away from the nice hospital you put him in and kills Laval, I suppose I ought to order the men to treat him nice when they can catch him so's he can knock off somebody else. Sick!"

"He said he was after the C.O. and Colonel North," Keene put in from his place near the doorway. "Didn't he, Major?"

Denver shot a glance at Hugh and then nodded slowly. "But he was very disturbed," he explained. "He probably didn't know what he was saying."

"But he did say he was out for me as well as Colonel Flood?" North asked curiously.

"Oh yes. I was trying to restrain him, you see, and he was muttering something about having to get Colonel Flood and you, Colonel North. Then, when I had him quieted, finally, he pulled out this gun he had hidden somewhere on him and let me have the barrel alongside the head. Out the window he went, screen and all, just before I blacked out."

"What kind of a gun was it, Major?" North asked.

Denver opened his mouth to reply, and the words stuck in his throat. He cast one brief, agonized glance at Jack Flood and then forced himself to meet North's eyes.

"I don't know," he said. "It all happened so quickly."

And what's the connection between a .28 caliber, a woman's gun, and Jack Flood? Another thing: How could Cagnieri have known who I was when he was stretched out unconscious at the time Flood spoke my name to Laval? The latrine grapevine? Or was Cagnieri really out?

He turned to Colonel Flood. "Who sounded the alert?"

"I did. Why, wasn't I supposed to? My God, I had a post that was runnin' around in circles with everybody yellin' a crazy killer was loose—my O.D. didn't seem to be doin' anything about it—of course I told 'em to sound the alert. What else? I had to get my men back under command."

North bought it, even though the alert had made it easy for Laval's killer to get away. His next question was addressed to Major Joe Denver.

"Did you know Laval was a drug addict?" he asked. "I heard you say his troubles were over—did you mean his troubles with dope?"

"No," Denver said. "I didn't know he was an addict. I meant his—er—deviate tendencies. You see—you see, Colonel, Laval came to me not long ago. The chaplain who was here was invalided back to Manila with malaria six months ago, and since then I guess I've served as a sort of father confessor to some of the men. The Hippocratic oath and all that. Well, Laval said he was afraid he'd—well, he had a terrific problem, Colonel; I can tell you that without violating confidences."

"But you didn't know he was an addict?"

"No, but I'm not too surprised," the post surgeon said. "As Colonel Flood will tell you, we had a robbery a couple of weeks ago in my dispensary; the strongbox containing my narcotics was rifled, but nothing else was taken. That pointed to an addict among the men."

"We had a shakedown," Flood said. "We didn't find anything. This has always been a bad place for junk, anyway. I guess a hophead could get all he needed almost anywhere among the gooks for a coupla bucks. We've got it almost stopped, but you can never clean it all out."

There was a new arrival at the doorway to the office. Kenny Trotter stood there with his pistol on his hip and North's gun and holster in his hand. He said nothing, but the relief in his eyes when he saw his colonel told North that the word was out at Fort Winfield that a crazy man was loose, gunning for a G-2 colonel.

"Had trouble getting here, sir," Trotter explained as he handed North his gun. "Seeing I was a stranger to the guards and with the alert on, it took me some time to get out of the castle."

"You shouldn't have got through at all," Flood complained. "Keene, what kind of orders have you got out on this alert, anyway?"

"You forget, Colonel Flood, that I passed the O.D. over to a new officer at guard mount," Keene said with furious, silky respect.

"Well, who's got it?"

"Captain O'Hare, sir," the other officer said.

"It would be Bottles," the C.O. grunted. "With that alky handlin' the guard we might as well say good-by to Cagnieri right now."

"Oh, Bottles was in good shape," Major Denver said placatingly. "A little excitement like this is what he needs to snap out of it. Sober, he's one of the best officers on the post, if you want my opinion, Jack."

Flood stared sourly at the medical officer. "Which I don't," he said, point-blank, and then gestured toward Laval's body. "Well, somebody get this hophead out of here before the heat gets him and he stinks up the place." The utter callousness of the man struck even the case-hardened North with something of a shock, and Kenny Trotter frankly winced, but neither Keene nor Denver appeared surprised; evidently duty at Fort Winfield under Lieutenant Colonel J. J. Flood had dulled their sensitivity in a good many ways.

Flood lumbered toward the door, grumbling, "Another goddam investigation—first Coulson and then the dope robbery and now this shootin'. And that gook in Zamboanga, too. And I've got to find Cagnieri somewhere on an island that was made for hidin' out, and in all this heat. Feels like a real blow's comin', too— we'll prob'ly wind up with havin' another typhoon like we had in '51, just to fill out the hand."

At the threshold, the broad-shouldered C.O. stopped as though tapped with a reminder. He turned slowly and faced North, his eyes somehow defiant.

"You'll prob'ly think I'm nuts, Colonel," he said, "but when we got the word from Zamboanga that you were comin' over here, my wife made arrangements for a little party in your honor. It's gonna be tonight."

Despite all his training, North had to gape. "A party!" he exclaimed.

57

"Yeah," Flood said uncomfortably. "I know it sounds dizzy but"—his manner changed to something close to pleading—"jeez, Colonel, you don't know what it's like on this post for a woman like Estelle. She—she's used to a lot different and—and, well, maybe you can see how she'd grab any excuse to live a little, dress up, have a party. She don't see hardly anybody but the people on the post from one year to the next, and when somebody comes to Winfield from the out-side . . ." He waved two big hands in a helpless gesture.

"Well, you know," he ended lamely.

"But, Jack, with Laval murdered and Cagnieri loose —you can't be serious," Major Joe Denver protested.

"That ain't gonna make any difference," Flood said stubbornly, his jaw jutting. "Laval won't be any deader if Estelle has her party, and Cagnieri won't get caught any quicker if she calls it off." His eyes sought North's again, filled with that strange plea. "I know you rank me, and you can tell us all to go to hell," he said, "but —but you'd be doin' Estelle and the other women a big favor if you'd okay the party. You'd only have to show for a couple of minutes if you've got work to do and—it'd mean a lot to my wife, Colonel North."

Hugh North's smile was immediate and warm, no matter what misgivings lay behind it. "It's as you say, Colonel." He nodded. "Mrs. Flood's party can't make any difference to Laval, and if it won't affect the search for Cagnieri, I think it would be a fine idea."

He barely heard Kenny Trotter's smothered ex-clamation. Yes, he told himself, it must look odd, to say the least, for a G-2 colonel on one of the most urgent cases in the Open File of World War Two to agree to a silly officers' wives party a minute or two after a key figure in the case had been shot before his eyes. But the fact was that this investigation had been brought to a temporary but complete stop right here. Cagnieri was somewhere out in the black jungle of Sanga Sanga, presumably with the gun that had killed both Paul Laval and George Lee—if it was the same .28; ballistics would tell that even though it would take time. Laval was silenced forever, and so was Lee, and by the same hand, no matter how hidden that hand might be at this time.

That was the theory that Hugh North must proceed on, that even though Laval, the baby-faced drug addict, had shot Lee down, and supposing that Cagnieri, a psycho made violent by the heat and Flood's persecution, had killed Laval, there was somebody—and somebody *here*, on Sanga Sanga—who had arranged both murders. Cagnieri's killing of Laval could be grim coincidence—the deranged soldier could have shot the hired killer blindly—but Hugh North thought not.

So, until daybreak or until Cagnieri was caught, there was no direct action North could take in the Hansen case. What better way, then, to spend part of this meeting than talking to, sizing up, the people of Fort Winfield, officers and wives, any one of whom might be the evil genius who had to kill and kill to keep from being exposed to the world as the worst of all human scum—the traitor?

"Yes," Hugh North said firmly, "I think the party is just what we need."

ii

Colonel North and Lieutenant Trotter were the last
guests to enter the Floods' quarters in "Killer Castle"
that evening, and they found the party in full swing,
all incongruities surrounding the affair apparently forgotten.

As North hesitated at the threshold, a slender figure
in white detached herself from a small knot of uni-
formed men—Keene, Denver and another officer—and
came toward him, hand outstretched.

"Colonel North!" she exclaimed. "So very nice of
you to agree to this little party in spite of the dreadful
thing that's happened." She came close to him and
looked up with blue eyes that would have been beautiful if they had not been so strained, shadowed. "I'm
Estelle Flood," she said and looked beyond North at
Kenny. "And you must be Lieutenant Trotter. How
d'you do, Lieutenant?"

While Kenny was bowing over Estelle Flood's hand,
making small talk, North studied the C.O.'s wife. The
first thing that struck him about her was her contrast
to the man she had married. Either she was younger
than Flood by twenty years or she had a good beauti-
cian—and the yellow pages of a Sulu Archipelago
directory must list mighty few beauty shoppes.

And that complexion, that shining cap of ash blond
hair, the curvesome body under the white dress—these
were no products of creams or lotions or dyes or

falsies. Estelle Flood was a lovely creature—or she would have been if she were not so nervous, so taut. So scared.

Scared of Cagnieri? Scared of my being here on Sanga Sanga?

He laughed mirthlessly behind his mask. *If I asked her why she looks this way, she'd probably blame it on the heat. Everybody here blames everything on the good old heat.*

"I know you must think I'm ridiculous, having a party at a time like this, with poor Paul just killed by that awful crazy man," Mrs. Flood was saying. "But I felt I just had to—to see you, Colonel." Her smile was bright—too bright. "Oh, I haven't any terrible crime to confess, Colonel, but it's so wonderful to have a visitor from the civilized world that I couldn't let you leave without meeting you."

Sure you haven't something to confess? Then why the guilt under the fright, little girl?

"And the others are just dying to meet you, too," Estelle was saying, "so let me introduce you." She tucked her hand in North's proffered arm, and Hugh could feel the tremor of her fingers, even through the light cloth of his blouse. This girl was close to a crack-up.

"Janice," Mrs. Flood said, "this is Colonel North, Mrs. Coulson."

An older, richly tanned woman with a striking streak of white marking her warm, neatly coiffured brown hair looked up from her chair. No scarcely hidden fear here; Janice Coulson had a mature comeliness that was made more attractive by her quiet ease of manner.

Her smile, her voice, bespoke the mature mind, able to cope with life with a minimum of the tensions that seemed to breed on Sanga Sanga.

This, then, was the widow of Captain "Creepy" Coulson who, to quote Keene, had "done the commit." As he took her hand, North looked hard at Janice Coulson and saw a woman he had known—how many years ago?

She saw his recognition, and her smile widened delightedly. "You remember, Colonel," she crowed. "Yes, you knew me when I was Harry's wife, Harry Crooks. You were a captain then, I think."

"Of course"—he nodded—"and Harry had just . . ." His words were drowned out by a pealing crack of thunder, the roar of a tropical shower that thundered down outside. Hugh North had never quite gotten over his surprise at the sudden fury of the storms these latitudes brewed or in their abrupt endings; one moment it would be clear, the next it would be teeming, and then, in another minute, it seemed, it would be clear again.

While he waited for the first tumult of the storm to subside, Hugh thought back to Harry Crooks, the first husband of this handsome woman who was now the widow of Captain Forrest Jackson Coulson, who had been known as "Creepy."

He had met Janice in Manila in 1940, and Harry was celebrating his rise to major in the old Army Air Corps. Hugh had been in the Philippines on the trail of a deserting officer who had absconded with company funds (Lord, how picayune those jobs really had been when they had all had Pearl Harbor hanging over their heads, a little over a year away!), and his search had brought him to Clark Field and the new Major Crooks' wild celebration.

Good old Harry, a screwball, perhaps, but a good flier and a brave one; they were always pinning flying medals on him, even in peacetime, when they weren't threatening him with court-martial for his off-duty escapades. An inveterate gambler, a hard drinker, he had nevertheless been wholly devoted to his wife, this woman who smiled up at North now. Harry Crooks was gone, killed ten days after Pearl Harbor in one of the few planes that had gotten off Clark Field (and how had that mess ever happened, after the bitter lesson taught at Pearl?) when the Japs swept down on the Philippines.

And after life with a gay screwball like Harry Crooks, how come Janice had married somebody who had earned the nickname "Creepy," an enlisted man commissioned in the field?

The storm slackened enough to allow conversation, and North and the widow spoke of other days in Manila, Old Army days when the Air Corps was the stepchild of the services and air power was not the biggest thing in national security. In the midst of this "remember when" session, North felt a slight tug at his arm.

"And this is Manuela Rickerson, Colonel North," Estelle was saying. "You've met her husband, Lieutenant Rickerson, I believe."

Manuela Ortega Rickerson had deep, deep eyes, a tea-rose skin, sharply aquiline features, hair of fine-spun ebony, a spectacular figure cunningly displayed.

Her Spanish ancestry showed plainly, but none of the
Moro blood that North knew had run in Ortega veins
by intermarriage since the turn of the century. Oh yes,
he knew quite a bit about the Ortegas, especially this
girl's father, Esteban Ortega, did Colonel Hugh North.

Manuela Rickerson suspected that he did, too, by
the chill defensive attitude she took on sight. She murmured only a brief word before she turned, with a
rudeness that was incompatible with her beauty, and
walked away, across the room to her husband.

"Oh, dear," Janice Coulson murmured, "that was
quite unwise, my girl." Her fine brown eyes upturned
to North's. "You mustn't take that the wrong way,
Colonel—Manuela must think you're here to rake up
that old business about her father." There was a glint
of speculation in her stare. "And you're not, are you?"

"Heavens, I hope not," Estelle Flood said nervously
before Hugh could reply. "Manuela's suffered enough
because her father was a Jap collaborator." The shadowed eyes of the C.O.'s wife met Hugh's, then looked
away. "She wasn't to blame for any of it, no matter
what they say," she muttered. "She was only a child
when it all happened."

"Only sixteen or so." Mrs. Coulson nodded. "Lord,
she was no spy, even though her father was—or so they
said."

*A sixteen-year-old is a woman in these parts. Hansen
used them that young in other places.*

"Probably she's had another squabble with Rick,"
Janice Coulson said quietly. "Those two—I was afraid
it wouldn't work when Rick asked my advice."

"Recently married?" North asked idly.

64

"Eighteen months or so," Mrs. Coulson said. "It would have happened much sooner if official permission hadn't been held up so long. Somebody in your headquarters must have thought it wasn't such a good idea for a spy's daughter to be married to an officer of the United States Army."

"But—but nobody *proved* Ortega was a spy, did they?" Estelle asked.

North was saved from the need of answering by the boisterous arrival of another woman, who, by the process of elimination, must be Mrs. Bottles O'Hare. And what a lot of woman!

Anne O'Hare (Keene had called her "Annie," and it fitted her) was something off the stage of a theater that would just have to be called The Gayety; she had all the lusty brashness of a burleycue soubrette. She was big, hearty, slightly blowsy, with a mop of suspiciously red hair, a frankly displayed bosom that had been chalked white for the occasion, a great deal of jewelry, an overapplication of rouge and lipstick, and a hiya-fellers attitude that was refreshing to North after Estelle's nervous tension, Manuela's antagonism and the general atmosphere of suspicion and hate on Sanga Sanga.

"Hi." She grinned at the G-2 colonel as she pushed in front of Janice Coulson's chair. "Bottles told me you were good-looking but he's usually such a liar I didn't really expect much." She looked North up and down with frankly appraising eyes, then turned to Mrs. Flood. "For gawd's sake, Stelle, you been draggin' this poor guy around, introducin' him to everybody, without givin' him a drink? C'mon, Colonel—I'll buy."

Before he could have protested, even if he would,
Hugh found himself being propelled across the room
toward a bar where a thickset man in a white jacket
handled drinks with a professional hand.

"Meet Jimmy Mulcahey," Mrs. O'Hare said, with
an expansive flourish toward the bartender. "Old
cavalry, Jimmy is, and they don't mix 'em any better
than the cavalry, I always say."

Mulcahey, the latrine-orderly–bartender, smiled
with a flash of gold teeth. "Missus O'Hare is a great
kidder, Colonel," he said. "What'll it be, sir?"

"Jimmy"–North smiled back–"would you know
how to fix a real gimlet?"

"Yessir," the bartender said matter-of-factly, and
did things with gin, lime and a frazzled bamboo
swizzlestick, no ice. North sipped cautiously and then
beamed; all was not middle-of-nowhere on Sanga Sanga.

As he savored his drink, Annie O'Hare suddenly
dragged him a few steps away from the bar and began
slurring talk at him in a muted, rapid-fire monotone.
"Look, Colonel," she said, "I wanted to talk to you
before these other bastards got to you–that's why I
took over. Look, I know they're gonna throw Bottles
to the dogs, the crumbs, but he's all right, Bottles is.
Sure, maybe he drinks too much, but he never, by
God, did a mean thing in his life, drunk or sober. And
Jack Flood better not try to make him the patsy in
this mess, either."

"My dear Mrs. O'Hare," North said, as quietly, "I
don't know what you're talking about."

"Yes, you do," Annie said, breathless now in her

66

hurry to have her say before they were interrupted. "Everybody says you're here about some guy that was knocked off in Zamboanga or on account of that kid Laval, but I'm bettin' you're here to find out about what happened to Creepy. Well, go ahead and find out, but don't let 'em put Bottles in the middle. They'll try to—they're already tryin' to. Didn't they put Bottles on O.D. tonight when it wasn't even his turn just so they could get him out of the way while they gave it to him?"

"It wasn't Captain O'Hare's turn on O.D.?"

"Naw, hell, he had it just a coupla nights ago. They're out to get him. Look out for them, Colonel. Look out for everybody on this damn island—*everybody!* Look what happened to that little sissy-britches Laval, Estelle's pet poodle. And Creepy—look what they did to him!"

"What did they do to Captain Coulson?" Hugh wanted to know.

Annie O'Hare's eyes slid around the room, returned to North's. "Janice knows," she whispered, "but she's afraid to talk. All she wants to do is get off Sanga Sanga before they do something to her. I don't blame her."

"I still haven't found out what you think happened to Captain Coulson. You mean he was driven to suicide?"

"Suicide, my foot!" Mrs. O'Hare snorted. "Creepy didn't shoot himself. He was murdered, that's what!"

"Mrs. O'Hare," North rapped out, "you know what you're saying, don't you?"

"Yeah, I know, all right." Annie stopped her head-

67

swiveling long enough to pin North with a direct stare. "Maybe I can't prove it, but the story that Creepy killed himself is all baloney. Why, the day before he—"

She broke off, looking beyond Hugh, her full, painted mouth halted in mid-chatter.

"Colonel North," drawled a slow voice over Hugh's shoulder, "have you got a minute, please, sir? Manuela and I have something important to tell you."

North turned to confront the lanky, Gary Cooperish Lieutenant Arthur Rickerson. He nodded, turned back to excuse himself from Annie O'Hare with a promise to see her later, to hear her complete story. Bottles O'Hare's wife was gone. She had scuttled across the room to Captain Pat Keene like a scared rabbit.

North turned back to Rickerson and the lieutenant's beautiful, cold-eyed wife.

"Is this place all right to talk?" he asked.

Rickerson looked about the room and shook his head. "Out in the corridor would be better, sir."

When the door to the Floods' quarters had closed behind them, Rickerson looked at his wife for a long moment, as though expecting her to do the talking, and then spoke hesitantly.

"I—Manuela didn't want to bother you," he said, "but I reckon you'd find out sooner or later, so it'd be best to have you get it from us."

He drew in a deep breath and blurted, "Manuela thinks young Laval was shot with her pistol."

iii

Hugh North had had long training at hiding his surprise; he needed it now to keep himself from blinking.

"So?" he managed, calmly enough. "It *was* a woman's weapon that killed Laval, you know. Suppose you tell me about it, Mrs. Rickerson."

Mrs. Rickerson was not telling anything, at least not immediately. She kept her black eyes fixed in an aloof stare down the hallway; her velvety lips were firmly closed and stayed that way.

Hugh waited and then said, "Well, suppose you tell me about it, then, Lieutenant."

"You tell him, Manuela," Rickerson burst out. "For God's sake, forget that tripe about Colonel North being here to go over your father's case again! Tell the colonel what you told me."

The enormous eyes surveyed Hugh North icily, the perfect mouth opened, the soft-spoken words emerged, only faintly accented.

"I didn't think my husband would rush to you with what I told him in confidence, Colonel North," she said, "but as he apparently wants me to put a noose around my own neck, I'll do what he wishes."

"You won't be putting a noose around your neck," Rickerson snorted impatiently. "Colonel North's no gestapo, for the love of Mike!"

The young woman's eyes flicked at her husband before they came back to North.

"The secret police have many names," she murmured. "I imagine their methods are very much alike, no matter what they're called."

"Manuela!" Rickerson said in a despairing voice.

"Suppose you tell me about the pistol," North suggested. "You think it was your .28 that killed Laval?"

She shrugged her creamy shoulders. "Very probably," she said. "I own a gun like that—or I did. It was stolen." Her dark eyes held steady on the colonel's. "I suppose the story of the stolen gun is an old one to you, Colonel. This time it happens to be true."

North nodded, his mind busy. Why would Major Denver lie (after an anguished glance at Jack Flood) about a gun stolen from Manuela Rickerson?

"You reported the theft?" he asked.

She shook her head slowly. "No. No, I—I thought that somebody had—borrowed it and would put it back."

"Rather an unusual possibility, don't you think?" North asked. "Perhaps you mislaid the pistol, lost it, and hoped you'd find it later."

"Perhaps," Manuela Rickerson murmured, almost disinterestedly. "I don't know exactly what I thought."

The lanky lieutenant broke in, his voice still charged with impatience. "That's nonsense," he told North. "My wife just told me a few minutes ago that the gun I gave her was missing from her bureau drawer. She said that when she heard Laval was shot with a .28 she went to check her gun and it wasn't there." He turned to his wife. "What's the idea of making it sound like it happened a while back?" he demanded. "You just found it out, didn't you?"

Her eyes dropped. "No," she admitted, "it did happen a while back—about a month ago. I didn't tell you because—because I thought it would be returned."

"By whom?" North shot out. "Who did you suspect was the—ah—borrower?"

The smooth shoulders moved in another shrug. "It could have been anybody in the castle," Manuela said. "We never lock our doors, you know." He saw her lips twist in an acid smile. "No, we're all officers and gentlemen and the wives of officers and gentlemen, so why lock doors? We're always borrowing things from one another; why not a pistol? Perhaps somebody wanted it to shoot a snake or—or merely felt the need of a pistol for—for a rat or something like that."

"This is ridiculous," Rickerson grunted. "Who'd take a pistol out of your bureau without asking unless he was a common thief? Shoot a snake or a rat? There are a dozen rifles and pistols around this place—every officer in the battalion has his own side arm."

"But the side arm is a .45, not a .28," North pointed out quietly. "Perhaps the one who killed Laval needed a gun that would hide better than a service pistol. Also, there's the matter of ballistics. A service pistol would be easy to check." He asked Manuela, "Was your gun registered here at the fort, Mrs. Rickerson?"

"No," her husband answered. "It was a cheap little Jap-made gun that I bought in Zamboanga one day when I was over there. Manuela had been saying she . . ."

Now it was his turn to freeze up. "I just thought it

71

would be a good idea for her to have a gun," he finished lamely.

"Why don't you tell Colonel North?" Manuela asked. "Why don't you tell him I wanted a gun because I was afraid that friends of my father might kill me?"

Rickerson's lean face was ashen beneath the tan as he turned to North. "I suppose you know all about Manuela's father, Esteban Ortega," he said.

"Yes." The G-2 colonel nodded. To the girl he said, "Did any of your father's old associates ever threaten you? Have they contacted you since the war?"

She shook her head, but the former cold reserve was gone. "Not directly," she said, "but there have been—indications that they're uneasy about how much I might know."

Rickerson's voice was harassed. "It's all imagination, I tell you, Manuela!" To North he explained, "She thinks she's being watched, sir; she swears she's being followed every time she leaves the castle, even for a walk or a trip to the beach." He gave a harried wave of his hand. "I keep telling her it's the heat."

Oh, sure. The heat.

North eyed the girl, asking himself whether the burden she so obviously carried was shame and guilt over her traitor father or hate for those who had dealt with Esteban Ortega. He made his decision.

"Mrs. Rickerson," he said, quietly, intently, "please believe I'm your friend. I think I know how rough things have been for you because of your father's—sins."

72

Her rounded chin lifted higher. "I've never complained, señor," she said proudly.

"No, but my information is that it hasn't been easy for you. Your family's copra plantation was burned by the Japs when they evacuated Sanga Sanga; the Ortega fortune was stolen by the very people your father had served."

"That never was proved!" Manuela flared.

"I'm afraid it was, my dear," the colonel said gently. "Just as all our information points to the fact that you played no part at all in your father's operations. Of course, to be utterly honest, we could be wrong on both counts."

Manuela's head bowed suddenly. "I did not know," she muttered. "I swear I did not know he did such things."

Lieutenant Rickerson passed an arm about his wife's slender shoulders. "Of course you didn't, darling," he murmured. "Nobody thinks you did."

"They do," the girl said in a low voice. "They all think I was a spy—Annie O'Hare and her awful husband, Pat Keene, Estelle Flood, the colonel worst of all. That's why you haven't made captain, Ricky; Jack Flood hates me and he hates you for marrying me when he said no." She raised haggard eyes to Hugh. "Colonel Flood as much as told Rick that if he married me—a gook, as he calls us, and a spy's daughter as well—he'd make sure Rick regretted it. And he has, he has."

"Aw, Manuela, Jack makes a lot of noise, but he's all right," Rickerson protested. "Hell, I've gotten it as good as anybody at Winfield. Didn't he give me old Creepy's company when he could have—"

"Yes, he gave you Coulson's company so he could drive you to suicide like he did Coulson!" Manuela cried.

"He didn't!" Rickerson lashed out. "I've told you a million times never to say that!" He caught himself and looked at Hugh sheepishly. "Sorry, sir; this is Sanga Sanga's dirty linen. Go ahead with what you were telling Manuela. Perhaps she'll listen to you."

"It's just this, Mrs. Rickerson," North said soberly. "If you're motivated by any sense of loyalty to your father in hiding anything about his former associates, you're making a terrible mistake. We know your father was more or less trapped into becoming an Axis agent, and when the going got rough, these associates threw him to the wolves. They deserve nothing from you, Manuela—nothing but your deepest loathing."

"So many people have tried to make me name names," the girl murmured in a half-sob. "No matter how many times I say I never knew one of my father's friends in that spy ring they still think I do, that I'm protecting them." She flung out her hands toward the G-2 colonel, her shell broken at last. "Colonel North, if I could I'd give an answer to every question you could ask me about my father and what he did, whom he knew. I—my heart broke when he—when he was killed and the men who shot him, my own countrymen, told me he had been a spy for the Japanese all that time. But I know nothing, believe me. Nothing!"

Outside, there was the rumble of thunder as another storm swirled down about "Killer Castle," and Manuela started, looked over her shoulder down the dim length of the stone-walled corridor.

"But there are those who believe I do know things." She shivered. "They're here on Sanga Sanga, close to me. They wait and they watch and I'm frightened, Colonel North!"

She wept as she made her heart-rending confession.

"And sometimes, God help me, I'm afraid it's my own husband who is this evil, hidden creature. My own darling Ricky! Sometimes I fear he married me only to make sure I'd be close to him when this watching and waiting was ended and it was time to kill me!"

iv

"Manuela!" Lieutenant Rickerson cried in a horrified voice. "What are you saying?"

The Filipino girl swayed toward her husband, her tears streaming now, her full mouth working. "Oh, Ricky," she moaned, "take me away from this island, this wicked place. I've hated it ever since—ever since I've been old enough to know what it can do to a person."

The tall, lean officer caught the black-haired girl in his arms and held her to him tightly. "But you don't mean what you said," he murmured. "You couldn't."

"No—no, of course I don't mean it. I must be mad. But—but you—oh, there are always these poisonous doubts, these whispers, Rick! They say things without really saying them, with a smile and a joke, as if they didn't know how they cut me, how they eat away at me."

"Who says these things?" Rickerson demanded. "What do they say?"

"Oh, I suppose it's me," the girl said brokenly. "I'm the one to blame—I guess it's all part of being a spy's daughter. But when they wonder why you married a—a gook—"

"Don't say that word!"

"—when you had so many nice girls, American girls, society girls, in love with you, I wonder, too. Why did you go against Colonel Flood's orders, against everybody higher up, and insist on marrying me when even my own people warned you that I was fit only to be hated?"

"Because I love you, you dope!"

"And then when I told them about being watched, being followed, they did everything but tap their heads; I was crazy, they knew. They all laughed when they found out you'd bought me the gun."

"It was common knowledge that you had this gun, then?" North asked sharply.

Rickerson answered for his wife. "Sure. Jack Flood and Bottles and—oh, everybody kidded me about it. I remember somebody warning me I'd better not stray off the reservation with my wife owning her own gun. Joe Denver, I think that was, or Bottles." He patted Manuela's shoulder. "Darling, they were only kidding —when are you going to learn to see the difference between plain old American kidding and—and the other?"

"Never," said Manuela Ortega Rickerson brokenly,

"because they never—what-you-say—kid when they talk to me. They may make out they're joking, but underneath they're telling me that Esteban Ortega's daughter should go away; she doesn't belong with decent people."

"Now, Manuela, they don't mean that at all," Rickerson said exasperatedly. "They're just—"

"Anybody special who bothers you?" Hugh North cut in.

"No," the girl said, her voice muffled against her husband's chest. "No, it's everybody—or nobody. Maybe it's as Ricky says; I imagine things."

Hugh bent closer to the young wife's bowed head, so close that he could savor her exotic perfume. "Mrs. Rickerson," he murmured, "do you know where the wreck of the *Kinshu Maru* is? Speak softly when you answer."

Manuela straightened in her husband's arms and looked at North with wide, tear-dewed eyes.

"The *Kinshu Maru!*" she exclaimed. "That was the name of the ship that Father waited for—it was going to take us away somewhere where we'd be safe, Father and I. But it never came. It never came."

North swallowed his disappointment. "It may have tried to get here," he said, "but it was sunk near here. You don't know where, I presume."

Manuela's brow wrinkled. "No," she said, "but—oh, there was a night when there was a terrible explosion. It woke me up, it was so close. That was when the battles were first starting in the Sulu Sea, and I was frightened. I ran out of my room, looking for Father, but he wasn't in the house. I met him coming back

77

from the cliff overlooking the beach, and he was very angry, and sad, too. He never told me anything about what he'd seen, the explosion, but he never mentioned the *Kinshu Maru* again."

"Do you know what direction the explosion was in?" North asked.

"No, it wakened me, as I said. But my father must have been looking to sea on this side of the island if he saw it."

North asked his next question of Rickerson. "Are there any wrecks close by, Lieutenant? We flew around the island before we landed, but I didn't see any from the air."

The lieutenant shook his head. "None that I know of, Colonel. Not real close, anyway. There are a couple of wrecks near Zamboanga and a whole flock of them in the Basilan Strait where Kinkaid's Seventh Fleet massacred the Japs. But if there's a wreck close in to Sanga Sanga it must be plenty deep. The shore slopes off very steeply around here, you know."

North nodded gloomily. Until George Lee had headed for Sanga Sanga, G-2 had reluctantly accepted the theory that the *Kinshu* was lying on the bottom at sixty or seventy fathoms, together with Arnulf Hansen and his microfilm, plus a fabulous fortune in pearls. Japanese naval records had proved only that the old Chinese coaster had been sunk "near Sanga Sanga," and Lee had been the only known survivor, as far as G-2 knew.

When Lee dashed for Zamboanga, en route to Sanga Sanga, hopes had been raised that it was possible to reach the wreck of the *Kinshu Maru* by something

78

other than a multimillion-dollar diving expedition. But now, if Manuela and her husband were to be believed, this hope was gone, although the knowledge that the pearls and microfilm, at least, were not at the bottom of the Sulu Sea was established. Now North must proceed on the theory that the pearls and film had been secreted *on* the island, possibly put there by Lee somehow before he left on the Jap destroyer that was, in turn, sunk off the China coast.

And if they were hidden on Sanga Sanga, Hugh North told himself dismally, they were going to take some finding.

He began another question, but checked it as footsteps clattered on the stone steps leading up from the courtyard. The trio watched silently as the burly figure of Jack Flood topped the stairs and came toward them. The big lieutenant colonel squinted through the gloom until he recognized North and the Rickersons.

"Sorry I'm late to the party," Flood boomed. "Just came from checkin' Bottles and the guard. No luck on Cagnieri yet." He came closer and peered at Manuela. "What's the matter with you?" he asked bluntly.

Rickerson's wife turned away, hurried down the corridor to a door at the far end of the hallway and disappeared inside. Flood's bull head swung toward Rickerson. "You two been fightin' again?" he demanded. "I told you when you come to me, cryin' you had to marry that—"

"Easy," said the lanky lieutenant in a deadly voice. "Just take it easy, Jack."

Flood glared, his lower lip thrust forward, and then spoke to North. "I meant to tell you about her,

79

Colonel. Her name was Ortega, and her old man was Esteban Ortega, and I guess you know about *him*. Lousy, stinkin' traitor. The natives took care of him when the Nips pulled outta here, but Manuela musta conned 'em into lettin' her live, somehow, and Rick here fell for her line and—"

"Damn you!" Rickerson burst out furiously. "I told you the next time you made any cracks about my wife I—I—" He spluttered into silence.

Flood croaked a laugh. "Yeah, sure," he jeered. "You said you'd kill me." His thick shoulders jerked in another laugh, and he said to North, "Oh, I got me a fine, upstandin' staff here, Colonel. If they ain't threatenin' to kill me they're committin' suicide or gettin' plastered or just goofin' off on general principles."

"Why don't you transfer me out, then?" Rickerson sneered. "Why do you hang onto us if we're such a fouled-up bunch? Tell the colonel why, Jack."

Flood's scowl was venomous, but he did not answer. Instead, he turned to Hugh. "How come you're not inside at the party, Colonel?" he asked. "Hell, the guest of honor shouldn't be standin' out in the hall listenin' to certain parties tell him about the bogeyman that follows her around, spyin' on her."

"I was just going back," North said to cut off a further outburst from Rickerson. "I could do with another of Mulcahey's gimlets."

Flood's big hand was at his shoulder as North was steered back into the room where the party held forth. Rickerson stalked down the corridor to his quarters to comfort Manuela. Hugh saw that his aide, Kenny Trotter, had been captured by Annie O'Hare, while

Estelle Flood and Janice Coulson were chatting with Major Denver and Hilton Macy, the adjutant. The three junior lieutenants whom North had not met and in whom he had very little, if any, interest in connection with this case, appeared relieved to see Flood appear. As North headed for the bar and a gimlet, the trio of second Johns paid their respects to their C.O. and Estelle, and departed in a body. Evidently they were not so bored on Sanga Sanga that a party given by their battalion commander was more than a duty to be gotten over with as quickly as possible.

Perhaps they're scared of Annie O'Hare and can you blame them, North said to himself and then reproved himself for the thought. But unless he was mistaken, Mrs. Bottles O'Hare could be predatory enough to frighten nine young second lieutenants out of ten, bull-session boasting at the Point notwithstanding.

Flood ranged up beside him at the bar and tossed an order for a double bourbon and branch water at Mulcahey. There was no hint of camaraderie between the old cavalryman and the lieutenant colonel who had served more time as an enlisted man than as an officer. It was, North told himself, a curious thing how some field-commissioned officers were bigger snobs than the worst product of West Point. Jack Flood, it appeared, rated with the few whose noses tilted off balance the minute their shoulders felt the weight of officers' insignia.

"You meet everybody?" Flood asked North as they made way for Anne O'Hare, bound for a refill, Kenny at her side.

"Not those three second lieutenants," Hugh said, "but Mrs. Flood saw that I met everybody else."

Flood grunted and swigged his drink, eying the ebullient Mrs. O'Hare as Annie exchanged ribaldries with Mulcahey and Trotter's ears crimsoned. "She's gonna be plastered again before the night's over," the C.O. said. "She's as bad as her old man, Bottles. Dunno whether she slops it up so's she can put up with him or he stays in the bag so he can stand her with her playin' around with everything in pants. Guess it's a tossup."

He looked at North over the rim of his glass. "What line of bushwah was Manuela handin' you?" he asked, with no attempt at finesse.

North's *none of your damn business* died on his lips. "Oh, this and that," he said idly. "Maybe she mentioned something about a gun. A .28-caliber lady's gun."

He had not expected the reaction that he got. Flood's hand jerked violently, slopping his highball over him. The C.O.'s face went gray and his mouth dropped; his eyes went off balance with dismay.

"What'd she tell you?" he rasped when he found his voice. "How'd she know? Goddam it, *she's* always snoopin' around like a damn ghost—maybe it was her that—"

He stopped, his eyes fixed on his wife across the room.

"Well, so you know," he said, finally. "I s'pose you were bound to find out, sooner or later."

"Precisely what Lieutenant Rickerson said." North nodded.

"Uh, yeah," Flood said absently, and then brought haggard eyes up to meet Colonel Hugh North's. "Well," he asked, "now you know it was Estelle's gun that killed Laval, what're you gonna do about it?"

v

This time, Hugh North did blink. Within half an hour, forty-five minutes at the most, two men, each necessarily a suspect in this case by reason of his background, had said that his wife's .28-caliber pistol had killed Paul Laval and, therefore, George Lee.

A hell of a note. Usually, North spent a good deal of time trying to dig up ownership of a murder weapon, checking fingerprints and ballistics to establish whose gun it was; in this case, people seemed to be falling over themselves to claim the gun that did the deed—or rather to point the finger at their wives.

"You say the gun belonged to Mrs. Flood?" he asked, stalling for time and composure.

"Didn't you know?" Flood demanded angrily. "D'you mean Manuela was talkin' about somethin' else? But you said—"

"That she mentioned a .28-caliber revolver that was stolen from her bureau drawer some time ago," North broke in. "*She* seemed convinced that Laval was killed by *her* gun."

"Well—well—he must've been," Flood floundered. "I mean, I didn't know about her pistol bein' swiped, but if she says it was hers that killed Laval, why, that's it, ain't it?"

83

"And what about Mrs. Flood's gun?" North asked implacably.

The big lieutenant colonel glowered at him, furious for having blundered into this admission. For a while it seemed that he was considering a try at blustering his way through, giving North a "Who, me?" routine, but the chill eye of the colonel from G-2 discouraged this maneuver. Flood made an effort, though.

"It was prob'ly Manuela's gun," he said. "She knows a lot more about things that go on around this island than she lets on. Oh yeah, she says she didn't know what her old man was doin' all the time he was workin' for the Japs, but if you ask me—"

"I am asking you," North said pleasantly. "What about Mrs. Flood's gun? Or perhaps it would be better if I asked her."

Before the C.O. of Fort Winfield could stop him, North caught the eye of Estelle Flood across the room and raised a beckoning finger It was terrible manners, he conceded, but a C.I.D. operative could not bother too much with manners when there was a job to be done, and he could not afford to wait politely and thereby let Jack Flood speak to his wife alone.

"Dammit," Flood protested bitterly, "you don't have to scare her to death with a bunch of questions. I know all about the gun—I'd have told you. Don't say nothin' to her about it now, and I'll give you all the dope on it later."

"No deal," North said in a clipped voice and put on a smile for the rest of the room to see as the pretty, harried blond woman reached him.

"So here you are," Estelle Flood said with a brave attempt at gaiety that did not go with her eyes. "We were wondering if you'd escaped, Janice and I. We didn't see you anywhere, and Janice said suppose you'd—"

"Look, Stelle," Jack Flood said desperately, "I gotta go back and see how that hunt for Cagnieri's comin' along. Put the food on early, will you? Will you take care of it right away?"

"Why—why, yes," the slender woman said. "It's terribly early, though, Jack." To North she said, "We're all going swimming later, if you like, Colonel. Maybe we can get in a dip between showers—but even if it does rain on us, the rain's warm at this time of year." She seemed caught up in a compulsion to talk, as if she was afraid to stop lest somebody else talk, ask her questions. "Do you like to swim, Colonel North? It's about the only recreation we have here on Sanga Sanga. But we have to be very careful about sharks and morays and such things. Snakes, too, but not in swimming, thank heavens—the snakes are around the lagoon, and Jack has put the lagoon off limits for *everybody* ever since—"

She stopped short and, with eyes wide and her fingers stealing to her lips, she stared at her husband, the fright plain on her face.

Flood's ejaculation carried the impact of a curse. "Do I get somethin' to eat, for God's sake, or do I go hungry?"

"Oh, of course, dear, of course." Estelle Flood whirled and started away. North's hand shot out to touch her shoulder.

"Just a minute, Mrs. Flood," he said very quietly. "I called you over, remember? Would you mind telling me about your gun, the .28?"

For a second, he thought the woman would faint. Her cheeks went chalky, and her eyes threatened to go up out of sight under her lids. His grasp on her shoulder tightened to keep her from falling should she faint, but Estelle Flood recovered after an instant. Her color returned, and a weird sort of half-smile mounted to her lips.

"So you've found out about the gun?" she asked. "Jack was so sure you wouldn't, when I wanted to tell you. I knew it was wrong to try to hide it, but Jack said—"

"Listen, Stelle," Flood rumbled, "you don't have to tell him nothin'."

"Yes, I do," Estelle Flood said gravely. "I wish I'd gone against your orders, Jack, and told him as soon as I found out. This way, it looks as if I . . ." She swung around to face Hugh North.

"Yes, I had a .28-caliber revolver," she said. "I've had it for a long time; I took it with me when I left Manila in '41. It was my father's, and the last time I saw him he gave it to me and told me to use it—on myself if I had to."

"It was a .28?" North asked.

"Yes." The slight woman in the white gown nodded. "I don't know anything about guns, but I know it was a .28 because regular-issue ammunition didn't fit it; Jack told me the Army uses only .22- or .32- or .45-pistol ammunition. He had to get bullets for the gun over in Zamboanga after we had target practice in the

86

courtyard one day. That's the last time I saw the thing, when Jack got the new ammunition and loaded the gun for me. I put it—I put it in my dressing-table drawer, the bottom one where I keep things I never use. My junk drawer, I call it."

"And it was stolen?" North asked quietly.

Estelle's hands fluttered in an impotent gesture. "It must have been," she said. "I couldn't have put it somewhere else; I *always* kept the gun in that drawer."

"When did you miss it?"

"Jack came to me right after Paul was killed and told me it was a .28 bullet that had killed him. He said —he said that as soon as he found that out he thought of my gun, and we went to look at it and it was gone."

North considered. This had been the same story that Lieutenant Rickerson had told about his wife's discovery that her pistol had been stolen; when she had heard about Paul Laval being shot she had checked on her own gun and had found it had been stolen. But Manuela Ortega Rickerson had changed her story; later she had said that the gun had been missing for some time. Which was the true story? Why had she changed it?

He was about to ask another question when he saw Mrs. O'Hare and the post surgeon, Major Denver, coming up behind Mrs. Flood. Mrs. O'Hare quite evidently had paid more visits to the bar than most of the other guests; she was tight, and if she had been breezy before, she was loud now.

"C'mon, le's go swimmin'," she blared. "Y'r party's dyin' on its feet, Stelle. 'S too hot to sit around indoors, even in this mausholeum. Everybody wantsta go down t' the beach. Le's all go down t' the pavilion an' cool off." She grinned up lopsidedly at Hugh. "Y'like buck bathin' parties, Colonel North?" she asked.

Major Joe Denver rolled his eyes helplessly. "Annie, the irrepressible." He grimaced. "Somebody happened to mention that it might be cooler on the beach, and Annie took it as a mandate from the people to move the party. Actually, Mrs. Flood, it's a good party—don't listen to her."

"Dull's dishwater," the redhead insisted. "C'mon, le's go swimmin'. Bes' li'l swimmer on Sanga Sanga, tha's me."

"You go ahead swimmin'," Jack Flood said viciously, "and while you're at it, do me a favor and drown, will you?"

"You'd like that, wouldncha?" Mrs. O'Hare leered, swaying. "That'd get me outta your way, wouldn't it? Then I couldn't tell what I know, could I?" She thrust her liquor-reddened face up at Flood. "Go ahead, I dare yuh," she told Flood. "Throw me inna lagoon and feed me to the eels."

Mrs. Flood thrust out a hand. "Annie, don't say that, even jokingly!" she cried.

"You keep out of that lagoon!" Flood barked. "I mean it! I swear to God, Annie, if you go messin' around with them eels and get yourself in trouble I won't let anybody lift a finger for you!"

"What's this about eels?" Hugh North asked.

Flood explained gruffly, "That damn lagoon is lousy with moray eels—some of 'em twenty feet long or more. I lost a man a coupla years ago when he got smart and went swimmin' off limits. I ain't had any trouble that way since, except with drunks like Annie here."

He squinted at Hugh. "You know what a moray can do? You know what a dozen or a hundred or how many's in that lagoon can do? That wise guy found out, all right. There wasn't hardly enough left of him to bury."

"Don't, Jack." Estelle shuddered.

She had reason to shudder, Hugh North told himself. Of all the killers of the Sulu Sea, or any sea, the moray eel was the most vicious. The tiger shark might be the popular villain in most people's minds, but for killing instinct a big moray was a ten-to-one more dangerous creature.

"And you still go swimming in the bay, so close to the lagoon?" North asked curiously.

"Aw, they won't bother you." Annie O'Hare laughed. "Jack's got 'em trained to stay in his private lagoon. Anybody he don't like—heave-ho—into the eel pool with 'em, like they did in ancient times."

"Where'd you hear that?" Flood asked sourly.

"I read it in school," Annie retorted. "Don't you think I went to school?"

"Sure, sure. They had school in that home for delinquent—"

"Now, now," Major Joe Denver interjected smoothly. "Let's not let the heat get us and lose our tempers." He spoke to Mrs. Flood. "How about moving the party to the beach, Stelle? Annie has a point; it would be cooler in the pavilion."

89

"Are you nuts?" Flood demanded. "We got a crazy man, Cagnieri, runnin' around with a gun, and you want us to go down to the beach and make targets for him."

"Aw, Cagnieri's long gone," Annie jeered. "He's prob'ly over to Zamboanga by now—hitched a ride in a native boat or somethin'. Besides, Vince wouldn't hurt *me*; he's gunnin' for you, Jack, remember?"

Jack Flood's wide mouth twisted in a hard line. "You'd better hope Cagnieri ain't long gone," he told Mrs. O'Hare. "Bottles is O.D., and if he lets that crazy wop escape I'm goin' to make it really rough on that ginhead. If he was sober he'd have Cagnieri back in the can by now."

"He is sober!" Annie O'Hare flared. "He didn't have a drink before he went on duty. Don't you go around sayin' he's drunk, Jack Flood! I don't care if you are commandin' officer of this lousy missile base, you ain't gonna—"

"Annie, Annie," Major Hilton Macy said as he hurried up. "Behave yourself—you're spoiling Stelle's party. Janice says to come over and sit down and talk to her."

Annie swung bloodshot eyes toward the widow who sat at the far end of the room. "Won't do it," she muttered. "Won't shut up, even for her, and God knows she's the only friend I've got in this dump." She looked blearily at Flood. "When somebody like Janice Coulson thinks you're a louse, Jack, you sure-gawd must be, huh?"

"Goddamit!" Jack Flood grated. "Somebody get her out of here before I wring her fat neck!" He flung himself around and stalked away to a connecting door that led to the sleeping quarters, slammed the door behind him. There was a brief silence before Joe Denver said in a coaxing voice, "Come on, Annie. I'll get my bag over there and go swimming with you. Come on."

The blowsy redhead glared at the door through which Jack Flood had gone. "Damn big shot," she sneered. "He needn't think 'cause he made lieutenant colonel he can pull any of that stuff on *me*. I knew him when."

"Please, Annie," Estelle Flood begged softly. "Please go with Major Denver. We'll be down swimming later."

Mrs. O'Hare's hazy eyes swung back to fasten unsteadily on the younger woman's. "Promise?" she asked blurrily. "Y'ain't jus' sayin' that to get rid of me?"

"We'll go with you, Joe and Lieutenant Trotter and I," Hilton Macy said. "Give us time to change into our suits, and we'll meet you at the beach. I've got a pair of trunks that'll fit you, Trotter, and Colonel North, too, if you'd like to swim, sir."

"Later, maybe." North smiled. "I'd like to talk to Mrs. Flood alone for a few minutes."

Estelle Flood flashed him one brief, frightened glance before she nodded and resumed her pleading with Annie O'Hare. "You go ahead," she said. "I promise you we'll be down later. And, Annie, please, please, please don't go near the lagoon just to make Jack mad."

Annie O'Hare grinned her lopsided grin and reached out to pat Estelle's cheek. "You're a good kid, Stelle," she said. "Pity you're married to such a—a—" She drew in a deep breath to give vent to her description of Lieutenant Colonel John J. Flood.

"Come on, come on!" Hilton Macy said, and he and Joe Denver yanked, rather than led, Annie O'Hare out of the room. Kenny Trotter followed, after an inquiring glance at North and Hugh's answering nod.

There was a brief silence before Janice Coulson spoke from the bamboo couch where she was sitting. "Poor Annie," she said sadly. "She'll be so remorseful in the morning, too." She got up slowly. "And it's time old ladies were in bed, so I'll be going along, too, Estelle. Colonel North, I'll be seeing you before you leave Sanga Sanga, surely. Drop in on me—my quarters are in the other wing—and we'll do some more talking over of old times. Good times."

She waved away Estelle's protests, smiled at Hugh's promise to call on her for a long talk, and took her departure. As she opened the door to the corridor, Hugh could hear Annie O'Hare singing "In the Clover" with loud, if unskilled, enthusiasm.

Silence descended on the room again. Estelle Flood looked down at her hands, twisting a scrap of handkerchief in her long fingers.

"I've told you about the gun, Colonel North," she said nervously. "What else did you want to know?"

"Suppose you sit down, Mrs. Flood," Hugh replied gravely. "This might take a little time—I've got a lot of questions."

She took a chair and looked up at him, trying to summon her courage. "All right," she said, "what is it you want to know?"

"Several things," North told her. "For a starter, just how close were you to Paul Laval, and why?"

vi

Estelle Flood's face was tinged by a quick flush, but her reply was steady enough. "So you've been listening to Annie O'Hare, have you?" she asked.

"Suppose I ask the questions and you give me the straight answers," North said levelly. "I didn't have to ask Mrs. O'Hare anything about Laval and you. You've spoken of Laval as Paul a couple of times; he obviously was more to you than just another soldier in your husband's battalion."

Estelle looked toward the door through which Lieutenant Colonel Flood had disappeared and then down at her hands again. "All right," she said in a low voice. "I suppose I deserved all the talk that was spread about—about Paul and me. Yes, I liked Paul Laval—perhaps too much. But I—he—there never was anything between us except—except—" She floundered to a stop, then resumed with an effort. "He kissed me once," she said. "I know what you're thinking, the bored older woman playing around with a handsome child, but it wasn't quite like that."

Handsome child! Drug addict, cold-blooded killer, baby-faced monster!

"What happened," Estelle was saying, "was that I tried to do something to relieve the terrible monotony of this post for the enlisted men. You have no idea of how deadly it can be here. Guided missiles need no

93

particular maintenance work done on them every day like tanks or planes or—or cavalry horses. You can have just so much close-order drill and calisthenics and classroom lectures in this heat—you see I know my Army well—and the rest of the time is more or less a struggle to keep the men's morale somewhere near normal, at least. Off duty, unless they go to that terrible Zamboanga, what's a soldier to do? The U.S.O. does its best, I suppose, but—" She made a gesture of futility.

"So I got the idea that a little-theater group might be something to take the men's minds off the heat, the insects, the awful monotony. I'd had experience in amateur theatrics in Manila, and I thought we could —" She stopped, shaking her head. "I realize now that it was a silly idea, but at the time I was all enthusiastic. Pat and Rick and Bottles went along with the idea, even though they must have laughed at it among themselves. Hilton Macy and Major Denver were against it, but they didn't interfere. We all kept it from Jack because we knew he'd put his foot down on the thing out of general principles."

Her eyes came up to meet his swiftly. "You mustn't think I'm disloyal in saying that," she told North. "Jack's a wonderful person and a good commanding officer but—well, he'd never understand anything like that. I thought that later, when we got the thing going and put on a minstrel show or a farce he could laugh at, he'd go along with the idea."

"I see." North nodded and asked, "Laval was one of the men who signed up for these amateur theatrics?"

"Yes. He'd had professional experience in New York,

bit parts in TV, he said. Because he knew more than any of the others, I made him my assistant and we were together a lot. And perhaps I wasn't careful enough in keeping a—a distance between us. He was a very nice boy and—oh, I admit I was foolish. I didn't realize what I'd done until the day he—he kissed me."

She looked toward the connecting door again and added, "And Jack walked in on us."

Oh-oh.

"It was pretty bad," Estelle Flood said. "Paul was quick-witted, and I suppose he saved the situation from a scandalous scene. We had a lot of playbooks lying around—we were trying to choose our first production—and he explained to Colonel Flood that we were rehearsing. Jack didn't believe him, but he didn't do what I half expected him to; he didn't beat Paul up. Instead, he ordered him back to barracks, told him to keep his mouth shut, and later, when Paul was gone, told me there'd be no more of this craziness. He seemed more hurt than angry, really. It was the first he'd heard of the little-theater project, and I guess having me go behind his back, and all the others who had strung along with me, was almost as bad as finding his wife in another man's arms."

She fell silent again, and North prodded: "You didn't see Laval from then on?"

The woman in white hesitated, and then nodded reluctantly. "Yes, I did," she admitted. "Jack flew up to Manila on a call from headquarters and I—I arranged to meet Paul on the beach one night. Don't ask me why—I told myself I wanted to let him know that I was still his friend. I thought he needed a friend more than most, a woman friend. He was a strange boy, full of moods and inner conflicts. The other soldiers didn't like him. They laughed at the way he talked. They thought he was—well, you know." She stopped again.

"And so you resumed this—friendship?"

"No! No, Paul was changed. He had been such a sweet boy, but that night he was different, hard, swaggering, demanding, insulting. I had to almost fight my way off the beach. That was the last time I ever saw him."

"How well did Laval know Mrs. O'Hare?" was North's next question.

"I don't know," Estelle said primly.

"Come now," Hugh chided. "This isn't idle gossiping, Mrs. Flood; this is a murder investigation, remember."

The C.O.'s wife eyed the tortured handkerchief between her fingers. "Annie is completely reckless," she said, almost in a whisper. "She doesn't seem to care who knows about her affairs. Yes, she had Paul Laval on her string once. Paul's one friend, Cagnieri, too." Her voice was freighted with shame for Annie O'Hare as she kept on. "It seems that her husband doesn't care about anything except his drinking. Perhaps he's given up on Annie. When they first came here they used to have terrible fights about the way she played around, but lately Bottles just ignores it."

"What about Manuela Rickerson?" he asked. "Did she know Paul Laval?"

"Not that I know of," the C.O.'s wife said. "She's very shy. Besides, she hardly looks at another man,

96

she's so much in love with Rick. I'm almost sure she never had anything to do with Paul."

"Janice Coulson?" North asked, and as Estelle's indignant eyes flashed up, he smiled. "I'm not suspecting that Mrs. Coulson had an affair with Laval, Mrs. Flood. I just want to find out if she knew him."

Estelle considered. "I suppose she met him," she said carefully. "She does a lot of work with the enlisted men, especially at the station hospital. She's sort of a one-woman Gray Ladies. She's been a mother to a lot of homesick recruits, too. We're going to miss her when she leaves Sanga Sanga—sometimes I think she's the only *normal* person on the island—certainly the most comfortable person in Killer Castle. I—I think Pat Keene's in love with her. But to get back to your question, if she knew Paul it was only casually, as just another soldier."

Her eyes pinned themselves on North's, clouded by perplexity. "Why are you asking all this? Do you think one of us women killed Paul Laval?"

"The general idea is that Cagnieri killed him," North said. "With either your gun or Manuela Rickerson's—if still another missing .28 pistol isn't waiting for me at the next corner."

"Manuela?" Estelle asked. "She had a gun, too? But of course—Rick got it for her when she first thought somebody was spying on her."

"What about that?"

Estelle's reply was drowned out by a downpour, the heaviest of the evening. The C.O.'s wife waited until the first fury of the deluge abated, and then raised her voice to answer North's question.

97

"Oh, Manuela hadn't moved in here long before she told Rick that somebody was going through her things in their quarters, watching her in hiding, following her whenever she left the castle, spying on her inside the castle. Rick laughed at her, but finally he bought her a little gun to—well, to protect herself, I guess, in case this prowler or whatever you'd call it turned out to be real."

"She never said whom she suspected of watching her, going through her things?"

"Not to me. She keeps to herself so much that I don't think she'd confide in anybody except Rick."

"Do you think there actually was such a person?"

Estelle's forehead wrinkled. "I—I don't know," she said. "This castle can breed all sorts of fears in a person. I know I—I've thought the same thing, that somebody was watching me, wanting to do me harm. But I suppose it's the heat, the monotony. Jack swears that in Manuela's case it's only her imagination. He says she's suffered so much for what her father did that her guilt has given her delusions."

North's mouth twisted. "Colonel Flood said that?" he asked gently.

Estelle Flood crimsoned faintly again. "No," she admitted. "At least, he *said* it, but he was just quoting Major Denver. The way Jack put it was that Manuela was touched in the head. Jack doesn't like Manuela. He tried his best to keep Rick from marrying her, you know. He's convinced that Manuela must have known what her father was doing, even helped him. He can't forgive her for that, even though Manuela was only a child at the time, if she did know her father was a traitor and a spy."

That *only a child* bit again.

"Actually, Mrs. Flood," Hugh North said, "Mrs. Rickerson can't be so much younger than you."

The blond woman curved her lips in the first unforced smile North had seen on her face. "Thank you, sir," she nodded, "but you flatter me. I'm almost forty, and Manuela's twenty-eight, I happen to know."

"Then you were twenty-four when you left Manila?" North asked.

"And twenty-nine when I married Jack," Estelle supplied. "An old maid saved from lonely spinsterhood—or a woman who waited considerably longer than most for the right man to come along."

"How did you meet Colonel Flood?" The way in which the question was asked raised no resentment in Estelle.

"Annie didn't tell you that?" the C.O.'s wife asked lightly. "She would have if you'd talked to her long enough—with embellishments. The truth is, Jack helped me escape from Bataan. My family was in export-import in Manila, Colonel North; old Philippine hands. We had a lovely home on General Solano Drive, and I don't think there was a happier girl anywhere in the world than I was, growing up in that lovely place. Then, when Manila was bombed, my father and mother and two brothers were all killed and I—I guess I went insane from the shock. I don't remember anything until I found myself with a crowd of refugees on Bataan, trying to get transportation to Australia. I didn't consciously run away from the city; I think if

I'd been in my right mind I'd have stayed with my friends and neighbors and gone into Santo Tomas Prison with them. But, as I said, I found myself on Bataan, and Jack Flood, a sergeant who had just been commissioned lieutenant, helped me get on a boat to Australia. I guess he broke a thousand rules to get me aboard. He must have been quite ruthless. I was grateful. I wrote to him all during the war, and when it was over and I went back to the Philippines he found me and asked me to marry him, the first time he saw me. And I said yes."

"I see." North nodded. "Tell me, on Bataan when you met Colonel Flood, were any other men who are officers here now attached to the same outfit?"

"Oh yes." Estelle said. "It was a piecemeal affair, that regiment or division or whatever it was, and I was confused, but I remember that they were all there—Bottles and Rick and Macy and Pat Keene. I think Hilton was a lieutenant, too, but the others were still sergeants; they got their commissions later on."

"Major Denver?"

"Oh, goodness, no," Mrs. Flood said quickly. "Joe Denver has been in the Army only something like eighteen months. He frankly admits he pulled every string he knew to stay out, but the draft finally caught him."

"At his age?" North's eyebrows were up.

"Well, he looks older than he really is," Mrs. Flood said, "but even so, he's past the usual draft age, of course. He's never said much about it, but Jack thinks Major Denver did something underhanded to get a deferment one time and when the government caught up with him he had to volunteer to avoid real trouble."

She immediately amended this oblique accusation. "Jack told me that in confidence," she said, "and he said at the time that he might be wrong. All I know is that Major Denver's a blessing to have on Sanga Sanga. He might have fought against coming into the service, but since he's been here he's worked hard, both at his duty and at trying to make things a little easier for us all by his wit, his steadying influence, his never-failing good humor."

Colonel North nodded again. "Did he ever live in the Philippines before this hitch?" he asked.

"No. I think he comes from Connecticut, someplace called New Britain. Jack would know for sure."

North looked at the bedroom door through which Lieutenant Colonel Flood had slammed after his clash with Annie O'Hare. "Speaking of your husband, is he all right?" he asked. "I mean, I understand he has malaria attacks, and he's been gone some time."

"Oh, Jack went out the other door, the one that leads from the bedroom into the side corridor," Mrs. Flood explained. "I heard him leave not long after the others; I thought you knew, but of course you can't interpret the noises in this old castle."

"No, I thought . . ." North swiveled his eyes toward the jalousied living-room door as footsteps clattered outside. The knob turned, and Kenny Trotter, clad only in swimming trunks, burst through the opening.

"You'd better come to the beach, Colonel," he said in a torn voice. "Bad trouble."

Estelle Flood sprang to her feet. "Who is it? Jack?"

"No, ma'am," Kenny said, and swallowed hard. "It's Mrs. O'Hare."

"Shot?" North's question cracked across the room.

"No, sir," Trotter replied. He shook his head and passed a hand over his sweaty face. "No, she wasn't shot—or at least I don't think so. There isn't much to tell. The eels—the eels—"

Hugh North caught Estelle Flood just before her slumping body struck the floor.

Chapter Four

———————————————————

i

Colonel Hugh North looked down at what was left of Mrs. Anne O'Hare and winced. In all his years in a career that had seen many deaths by violence, he never had examined a corpse that had been so horribly mutilated. From the top of her head to the soles of her feet, the woman had been slashed and ripped until she was a mangled mass, which North was glad to cover again with the tarpaulin that had been brought by the medical corpsmen for a shroud.

He straightened, his frown telling Kenny Trotter, at least, that some impression other than stark horror had been raised by the examination. Overhead, the remnants of the most recent rainstorm bumbled away toward the northeast and the moon shone through to compete with the light of the gasoline lanterns that had been brought to the shore of the still, black lagoon.

There was a moment's silence, and then Bottles O'Hare asked in a tortured voice, "Is it all right to get her somewhere—somewhere where she won't be layin' in the mud?" The agonized grief of the big captain, who, to quote Estelle Flood, did not "care about anything except his drinking," was evident to all who heard him.

"Sure, Bottles," Major Denver said quietly, steadyingly. "Sure, you go on back to your quarters, and I'll be along in a minute to give you something that'll let you sleep. We'll take care of Annie."

The irony of his promise took a moment to sink through O'Hare's daze. Then the big man uttered a muffled groan. "Take care of her?" he choked. "Where was everybody when she really needed takin' care of?"

"Come on, old boy," Hilton Macy said, and threw an arm about O'Hare's shoulders. "Let's get back to the castle—I'll walk up with you if it's okay with Colonel North."

"Of course it's okay," Denver said. "I prescribe it. Here, I'll go with you as soon as I get my bag." He looked at Hugh and muttered, too low for O'Hare's ears, "When Jack yelled, the first thing I thought was it was lucky I'd brought my bag down to the beach with me. I thought it was a snake bite or something and then—then I saw Jack carrying her in to shore."

He looked at the canvas-shrouded corpse again, shook his head sadly and walked over to where his physician's bag sat, a few feet from where the officers and medical corpsmen were grouped. Then, with Macy, he helped the stumbling, weeping O'Hare out of the circle of light cast by the lanterns.

Hugh North looked at those who were left on the lagoon shore, five enlisted men led by a sergeant, Lieutenant Colonel Jack Flood, Kenny Trotter, Captain Pat Keene, Captain Arthur Rickerson. Flood and Rickerson wore soaked uniforms; the others were in swimming trunks, as Macy and Denver had been. All of those left at the lagoon were covered to their knees with swamp mud, all were insect-bitten and thorn-scratched. All showed the shock of this tragedy in their eyes, Jack Flood most of all, if horror could be measured in degrees.

North glanced again at the covered remains of Annie O'Hare and spoke quietly. "I've finished with my examination for now; you can have the men remove her, Colonel Flood."

The C.O. jerked himself free of his paralysis and gave a low-voiced order to the sergeant in command of the corpsmen's detail. The slain woman's body was placed on a stretcher and carried off.

"She'll have to be buried tomorrow," Flood muttered as he stared after the grim procession with haggard eyes. "Like poor old Creepy. In this climate you gotta bury 'em right away."

"Yeah," Keene said bitterly. "First Creepy and now Annie. I wonder who's next?"

The C.O.'s eyes swung slowly around to meet Keene's. "What d'you mean?" he asked. "You're makin' it sound like this is tied in with Creepy's suicide."

"Isn't there a connection?" Keene asked. "You hated their guts, both of them."

Flood seemed staggered more than angered. "That

ain't true, and you know it!" he cried in an anguished voice. "Didn't I cover for Creepy for months, years, when he oughta been Section Eight-ed out? No matter what anybody says, Creepy knows it wasn't *me* that made him do the commit!"

"You mean it was me, maybe?" Keene asked bitingly. "Or do you mean Rick or Bottles or maybe Janice? Was it us that rode him so hard, chewed him up whenever he pulled a clinker, threatened to have him court-martialed for things the poor guy didn't even know he was doin' half the time?"

Flood made a curious groping gesture with his big hands. "I didn't mean any of it, Pat," he said imploringly. "Maybe it looked like I was hard on Creepy—yeah, maybe I *was* tough on him. But you ask Janice, you ask Joe Denver; old Creepy couldn't keep goin' unless I kept on his tail. I didn't want to do half the things I did to him, but a guy in his condition *had* to be rode hard. Otherwise he'd get this what-you-call-it, melancholia, and crack up for sure."

"That's the damndest excuse I ever heard," Lieutenant Rickerson grunted. "And how about Annie? I suppose you treated her like you did so's she'd be a better woman, enjoy life more?"

Flood's head sagged as he shook it, slowly, doggedly. "No," he said. "No, I'll admit I hated Annie for what she did to old Bottles. Before she latched onto him, Bottles was a guy that could've gone places. She was the worst thing in the world for him. She dragged him down; she busted his heart, whorin' around the way she did. No, I admit I hated her. But I didn't kill her."

North stepped in again. "The eels killed Mrs. O'Hare, didn't they, Colonel?"

Flood seemed about to say something, but his teeth clamped down hard to lock in whatever it was. "It looks like it, don't it?" he asked, finally, and shuddered as he remembered the corpse that had just been removed. "Jeez, I wouldn't wish that on anybody. Not that."

Rickerson slapped at a mosquito and asked, "Can't we get out of this place and back to the beach where the bugs aren't so bad? This is murder."

"Yes," Hugh North agreed, "it is. And seeing that there doesn't seem anything to be done here before daylight and that I have some things to ask you all, let's adjourn to the beach."

"You'll have to wait with your questions," Jack Flood said bluntly. "I gotta get back to Estelle."

"She's in good hands," North said sharply. "Lieutenant Trotter and I got Mrs. Coulson and Mrs. Rickerson to stay with her. And these questions can't wait, Colonel."

The burly C.O. grumbled, but he went with the others to the beach where a soft, hot breeze kept the insects at a minimum. North led the men to a palm-thatched pavilion on the white sands and seated himself at the head of a bamboo table, waving his hand toward the benches. When they were all seated, the G-2 colonel leaned forward.

"Now I want the story and I want it straight," he said. For the first time the officers of Fort Winfield heard the spring-steel quality of Hugh North's voice that meant to Kenny Trotter, at least, that his colonel was nearing a showdown in this case. "I want you to go back to the party, when we were all together, and tell your story from there. Lieutenant Rickerson?"

The lanky officer told his story: "After Manuela and I talked to you and Colonel Flood came along, I went to my quarters to—well, to calm my wife down. She was all upset, you know. She told me to go back; she was afraid Jack Flood would make it rough on me if I gave Stelle's damn party the go-by." He turned to the lieutenant colonel as Flood muttered something under his breath. "Oh, Manuela knows you've got it in for me, all right," he said.

"Keep on with your story, Lieutenant," North said sharply.

"Sorry, sir. Well, I didn't want to go back to that crowd, where Jack could keep on burning me up. I'd heard Annie go singing down the corridor outside, saying something to somebody about going swimming, so instead of going back to the party I came down here to the beach."

"You saw Mrs. O'Hare?" North asked.

Rickerson's frown was visible in the semidarkness of the moonlit night. "I honestly don't remember," he told the G-2 colonel. "I was thinking about Manuela and—oh, I had a lot of things on my mind. There was a big thermos jug full of cocktails—it's still over there on that table—and I had a drink and sat down to try to figure things out—the pistol, Manuela's thinking she was being watched, whether she really loved me—all of it. I just said hello to a couple of people and sat there with my own thoughts. I suppose Annie was around when I first got here, but I can't be sure."

He stopped, trying to recapture a clear picture of who had been on the beach and when, then gave it up. "Anyway, I finished my drink and started back to quarters when I heard Jack yell from over by the lagoon. My first thought was Cagnieri. I ran toward the lagoon, and when I got there, Jack was wading out of the water with Annie."

He gulped at remembrance of that grisly sight. "There were a lot of people there by then, and—well, I guess that's it, Colonel."

North nodded and turned to his aide. "Lieutenant Trotter?" he asked impersonally.

Kenny Trotter told his story: "Major Macy got me some swimming trunks and I changed in our room. I came down here with the Major, and when we got here, Major Denver and Captain Keene and Mrs. O'Hare were in the water. We joined them, and after that some were swimming out into the bay and some were coming up to this pavilion for a drink, and I don't know where everybody was at any certain time, sir. Mrs. O'Hare was talking about wanting to swim in the lagoon just to be able to tell Colonel Flood he couldn't order her around. Major Denver and the others were trying to kid her out of it. I thought they had. Then, when I was out in the water, alone, I heard Colonel Flood yell from the lagoon. When I got there, he was about twenty feet out from shore, towing the body in. I helped him as best I could, and when he got Mrs. O'Hare ashore I went for you."

"How long had Mrs. O'Hare been gone from the beach here?" Hugh asked.

Kenny shook his head. "I don't know, sir. It could

have been half an hour; it could have been only a couple of minutes."

"You heard no scream from Mrs. O'Hare?"

"No, sir."

"Nor you, Lieutenant Rickerson?"

"I didn't hear anything out of the way until Colonel Flood yelled," Rickerson replied. "It had been raining hard off and on, though—Annie might have yelled, and we didn't hear her over the rain."

"All right. Captain Keene?"

Pat Keene told his story: "Annie was the first one down to the beach—at least she was here alone with her thermos jug when I got here. I tried to have her lay off the booze for a while; it's dangerous to go swimming at night with too much liquor in you. She laughed at me, of course. We swam around together for a while, but Annie was more interested in the drinks; she'd swim a little and then go ashore. She was right fried. Yeah, she was braggin' about how the morays didn't scare her and she'd like to go swimming off limits just to tell Jack that she had. I thought she was just soundin' off. She got too yackety-yack for me and, besides, she started to—well, you know Annie. When she had a load aboard she got ideas, and I didn't want any of that stuff—I got out of her reach."

His hard eyes came up to meet North's levelly. "That sounds like I'm slanderin' Annie, but it's the truth. I kept out of her way, like I always did when she was like that. Not that certain guys around here didn't do everything *but* keep out of her way when she was plastered."

"All right, Captain," Hugh sighed. "Let's not get another argument started. You avoided Mrs. O'Hare. Did you see when she left the beach to go to the lagoon?"

"No, sir."

"Did you hear her scream?"

"No, sir. Like Rick said, it was raining pretty hard for a while, but the first I heard was Jack yelling blue murder. Lieutenant Trotter said he was swimming alone, but I was out in the water, too—further out. Trotter beat me to shore, and when I got to the lagoon, Jack had Annie on shore and Trotter was just leaving to get you. I was pretty far out in the water when Flood yelled. I was the last one to get to the lagoon, I guess."

North turned to Lieutenant Colonel Flood. "And what about you, Colonel?" he asked.

Jack Flood came to again with a jerk and looked about dully, almost stupidly. Except for the flare-up that had followed Rickerson's charge that he had driven Coulson to suicide, the C.O. had been curiously silent, as though struggling with some deep problem. Now, when he spoke, his words came out slowly, with little inflection.

"When Annie burned me up, back there at the party, I went in the bedroom, like you all saw," he recited. "I laid down for a few minutes, but I was steamed up about a lotta things. My wife's gun. Manuela's gun. Laval gettin' knocked off by Cagnieri. What would headquarters say about me lettin' things like that happen, and right on top of Creepy's suicide, too? Hell, no wonder I couldn't relax.

"I dunno how long it was, but I finally decided to hell with Estelle's party—it looked like all I was doin' was foulin' it up, anyway. I said to myself I'd go down to the guard comp'ny's mess hall and scrounge a cuppa coffee and maybe a sandwich. Besides, I wanted to check up on Bottles, see if he was sober, find out if there was anything new on Cagnieri.

"I was goin' along the walk where it overlooks the lagoon and I heard somebody talkin' and somethin' that sounded like there was somebody swimmin' in the lagoon. I said to myself there's that damn Annie O'Hare doin' just what I ordered her not to, and this time I'll burn her tail good. I left the walk and cut over through the jungle toward the lagoon. It came down rain, hard, and I didn't have a light or anything; I had to double back, and I guess I lost my way in the darkness for a while. Anyway, it took me too long to get to the lagoon. When I got there—when I got there—"

He stopped and stared down at his hands, clenched on the table in front of him.

"When I got there, there was nobody swimmin'," he said, finally. "But out in the water was somethin' white I could just about see. I figured it was Annie; she'd spotted me comin' and she was tryin' to float real quiet so I wouldn't see her. But, hell, I said to myself, that ain't like Annie—drunk as she was she'd be givin' me a horse laugh. So she's in trouble, I said, and in I went, clothes and all, and swam out to her. When I got up to her and I saw her—"

A violent shudder rippled through Flood's thick body. "I yelled," he said, simply. "I yelled my head off, all the time I was bringin' her in." He stopped and studied his hands. "That's all, I guess," he told Colonel North.

There was another silence, broken by a distant rumble of thunder. Then the G-2 colonel asked abruptly, "Does Major Denver always carry his case along wherever he goes?"

"I can answer that," Pat Keene said. "Almost always. He's a nut on being ready for an accident. He told me once that back in the States he was out driving without his case along and there was a bad accident a couple of cars ahead and somebody died who might've lived if he'd had his doctor's case. Taught him a lesson never to be without it, he told me."

North stroked his chin, his brain busy. Then he said slowly, "I guess that's all for right now, gentlemen. You can go get some clothes on while I give the body another examination under some decent light. Lieutenant Trotter, you go with the others; I'll see you in our room."

The officers rose to their feet and started out of the pavilion. North's voice sounded quietly in the velvety darkness.

"Oh, Colonel Flood, would you mind staying a few minutes longer?" he asked suavely. "I've got just a question or two more to ask you."

Flood turned back obediently and sat down heavily. North waited until the others, Keene, Rickerson and Trotter, were out of earshot before he spoke.

"The *Kinshu Maru's* at the bottom of that lagoon, isn't it?" he asked quietly. "That's why you put the lagoon off limits for swimmers, isn't it, Colonel?"

Flood's mouth sagged, his eyes bulged.

"What d'you mean?" he asked. "I kept everybody outta the lagoon on account of the morays, like I told you."

"Ah, but, Colonel," Hugh North murmured, "you know there are no moray eels in that lagoon. You know Annie O'Hare was murdered by a human hand."

ii

For a moment, North thought that Jack Flood was going to do as his wife had done; faint dead away. The lieutenant colonel's mouth worked soundlessly, his eyes rolled, before he managed to get enough control over himself to speak.

"B-but you saw her, didn't you?" he asked hoarsely. "You saw what they did to her."

"I saw her," Hugh North nodded. "I examined her very thoroughly. Those wounds never came from a moray eel nor a pack of moray eels. Morays have even rows of sharp teeth, Colonel; they don't cut and slash —they tear chunks out of their prey. Those wounds were put there by a very sharp knife, used after Annie O'Hare was slugged in the back of the head. She never screamed, remember; she didn't make a sound. You heard her swimming in the lagoon from a distance; you would have heard a scream, rain or no rain. Oh yes, she was slugged. The wound is there, all right; I felt it quite distinctly when I was examining her."

This time, Flood's words refused to make themselves heard.

"Another thing, Colonel," North went on, "you said you saw Mrs. O'Hare's body floating out in the lagoon and you thought she was trying to be quiet so you wouldn't see her. If eels had attacked her, that water would be boiling. The eels wouldn't have left her until they had finished with her; a twenty-foot moray such as you said infested the lagoon could have and probably would have dragged her under and kept her there."

Flood's head dropped to his hands, but North went on inexorably.

"So you, the man who's warned everybody that the lagoon was full of deadly morays, plunged in and started swimming out to her without a second thought. You had no love for Mrs. O'Hare, but even so I guess your natural instincts would force you to try to rescue her, even if there had been eels. But it would have been a struggle; it would have been a terrible decision—facing death by those loathsome morays to get to Annie O'Hare. Yet you didn't mention any hesitation —no, you went right in, and it was only when you reached the body that you started yelling. Yelling? Perhaps screaming would be a better word. Because when you saw the mutilations, Colonel Flood, you screamed—*you thought then that there actually were eels in the lagoon!*"

Flood uttered a muffled groan.

"Suppose you give me the straight story, Flood," North said softly. "Did Annie know the secret of the

Kinsbu Maru? Did I tell it right, or did *you* kill her to keep her from blabbing?"

Flood's head came up, eyes staring widely. "No, I didn't kill her!" he cried. "I don't think she ever knew the damn ship was down there—unless she found it out just before she was killed."

"But you've known it was there for quite a while," North said. "How long?"

Flood wrestled with himself for a long moment, and then the dam behind which he had stored his guilty secrets broke, and the words came out with a rush.

"Let me tell it my way," he said. "First, I didn't kill Lee. Oh, I knew him—I guess you knew I knew him, even when I said I'd never heard of him. He was a loan shark, back in the old days, and he had half the guys in the Philippine service in hock to him, I guess. Then, when things got tight, he offered to cut the debt, even forget it altogether, if we'd give him a little information."

It took effort, but his eyes came back to North's.

"Sure, we should've turned him in—as if that would've done any good—but we thought he was a chump. You know what security was in them days, Colonel; we didn't know which end was up about security, none of us, from the top general to the newest recruit."

North nodded; that was too dismally true.

"The stuff Lee wanted didn't mean a thing—little picayune information. What battalion was movin' where, how many field pieces in which battery, stuff like that. Hell, we thought he was a screwball payin' good money for junk like that he could get in the newspapers, almost."

He reached into a pocket before he remembered he was soaked to the skin. Silently, Hugh proffered a pack of cigarettes; the lieutenant colonel took one and got a light from North.

."Thanks. Well, I was tellin' you about Lee. After Pearl Harbor and Bataan, of course, I knew what I'd done, who Lee was. I'd sold information to a goddam spy. Me, Jack Flood! And so had about every other guy in my outfit—my pals, Rick and Pat and Bottles— he was just plain Benny O'Hare then—and Hilton Macy and the others. You can imagine how I felt—a goddam traitor for a couple of lousy bucks."

He spat smoke angrily at the recollection.

"So after the war," the big man went on, "I married Estelle and I got this post. That was pure luck, Colonel —good luck or bad I don't know which. Anyway, I tried to get as many of the old gang that were left out here with me. I'll give you the straight dope on that. I knew I might be all right as a combat commander, but I couldn't pull a peacetime command without help. I'm a pretty rough guy, and you give me a bunch of officers out of West Point and O.C.S. and I'd never make it; they'd turn me in for what I am— a good sergeant, a lousy C.O. So I figured if I got my kind around me, guys that were drill sergeants like I was before they made officer, I'd do all right. I—I own me some medals that let me ask favors of the Pentagon, and I guess the top brass was glad to find somebody who'd stay on Sanga Sanga, so when I asked for Macy and Coulson and Keene and the others, I got 'em."

"Coulson, too?" North asked.

"Well, Creepy wasn't exactly one of the old gang. He was an Air Corps sergeant at Clark Field, but when the Japs knocked out the Air Corps, he joined up with us in Bataan. He made his commission as an infantry-man—he never went back with the Air Corps."

North nodded. "I get it, Colonel. Go on."

"Well, like I said, I got Macy and Keene and Bottles out here and I've kept 'em, too, even if they've done their damndest to get away. Maybe it ain't all selfish, either; they'd go nuts under a C.O. they couldn't call a sonofabitch once in a while to his face."

He dragged at his cigarette.

"Things were goin' along fine," he said, "and then about three years ago, Estelle and I were foolin' around the lagoon late one night. We—well, hell, we were skin-diving, and I do mean *skin*-divin'. Anyway, I went down deeper than usual, and I damn near got tangled up in this old wreck down there. Scared hell out of me. I didn't say anything to Stelle—she was always bawlin' me out for takin' chances in swimmin'—but the next day I went back and really looked that wreck over. I'm one hell of a good swimmer, if you want to know."

North, looking at the C.O.'s deep chest and broad shoulders, could believe it.

"I didn't tell anybody about it for fear it would get back to Stelle. I went down a coupla times before I could scrape away the weeds and stuff from the name plate on the bow. It said *Kinshu Maru*. Didn't mean a thing to me."

He paused again, puffing steadily, and then shot a glance at North.

"Here's where I prob'ly don't make much sense," he warned, "but this is the way it happened. One day Estelle followed me and saw me dive, and when I came up she gave me hell. So I kidded her, told her how there was a wreck down there, the *Kinshu Maru*, and maybe there was a load of gold in her and if I could get it, it'd be ours, so keep her mouth shut about it. I thought I'd conned her out of it, but one day about a week later she came to me, all upset, and said please, for her sake, stay away from the *Kinshu Maru*. Why, I ask her, and she won't tell me. No matter what I do, coax her, raise hell with her, she won't tell me. But you can see she's real scared about somethin'. She tells me that if I love her I won't ask questions, I'll stay away from the wreck."

He flipped his cigarette through the open side of the pavilion into the water that lapped the beach. Without a word, North offered him another and Flood took it, bent to take the flame from North's lighter.

"I ain't much of a one to show it," he told Hugh after a drag at the fresh smoke, "but I love that girl, Colonel. If she told me to jump off a cliff, no questions asked, I guess I would. I saw she meant it, so I promised what she asked; I quit divin' down to the *Kinshu Maru*. Then she said I had to keep everybody else from foolin' around that old wreck. Well, about that time one of the men ran into a moray or a shark, I dunno which, really, when he was swimmin' right at the entrance to the lagoon. That gave me a good excuse to make the lagoon off limits; I fed everybody a lot of guff about twenty-foot eels in the lagoon. Estelle helped me; she backed me up when I said we saw 'em, they chased us out of the lagoon."

Another puff at the cigarette.

"We said morays," Flood explained, " 'cause they don't show a fin like a shark. And, besides, a guy will be scared of a moray eel where he won't be especially panicked at the idea of a shark."

"And Mrs. Flood fainted when she heard about Mrs. O'Hare because she knew there were no morays in the lagoon; she knew Mrs. O'Hare had been murdered."

"Yeah, probably," Flood said. "But look, don't blame her for—for whatever's goin' on. I dunno what she found out about the *Kinshu Maru*, but whatever it is, it don't make her out wrong, Colonel. I'll swear to that!"

Estelle Flood, twenty-four when she left Manila, family in that convenient business, export-import. Why couldn't she have been a Hansen agent? She says she blacked out and found herself on Bataan; why couldn't she have known the Jap attack was coming and gotten away from Manila in time? She admits she was close to Laval—Flood found Laval kissing her—if Laval was her lover she could easily have gotten him to kill Lee. She owned a .28. It wasn't missed until Flood himself checked on it following Laval's murder.

Yes, Estelle Flood could stand some further questioning.

"About Annie," Flood was saying, "I think we're overlookin' somethin' important. How about Cagnieri?"

North hunched his shoulders. "I suppose he's a logical suspect," he said, "but I can't work up much enthusiasm for Cagnieri as the mad killer."

He glanced down the shore toward the lagoon, then looked up at the sky. "We've got some time, Colonel," he said, "and I'm afraid I'm going to have to ask you to stick close to me until dawn."

"Dawn?" Flood asked. "What happens at dawn?".

"I'm going down to the *Kinshu Maru*," Hugh North explained. "With luck, I'm going to find the answer to this whole case." And he smiled twistedly and added, "You'd think that with my experience I'd have given up hoping for good luck by now."

iii

Dawn was just streaking the eastern sky when Hugh North stepped up on the aft thwart of the rowboat propelled by Kenny Trotter at the oars and asked Jack Flood, "This is the place?"

Flood checked certain landmarks and nodded. "Right about here," he said. "You'll find the ship layin' over on her side. The door I went through to explore is toward the back, just behind the big hole in her."

North eyed the water and felt the knife and flashlight that hung at his belt. He glanced at Kenny; his aide was wearing his side arm, as ordered. Jack Flood was unarmed, still wearing his rumpled suntans; he had not changed since his soaking of the night before, neither had he shaved or eaten more than a few mouthfuls. The murder of Annie O'Hare had hit him hard.

"If only I hadn't cussed her out the last time I saw her," he had told North, a few minutes before. "Last thing I said to her was go out and drown yourself. It ain't a nice thing to remember."

. He had had no chance to talk with his wife, Estelle. Neither had North; when they had returned to Killer Castle, they had found that Estelle was asleep, under a heavy dose of sedation administered by Major Denver.

"She's on the verge of a nervous breakdown, that girl," the post surgeon told Hugh. "You'll have to wait until she's recovered from her shock."

So North, although he had burned to ask Estelle more questions now that he had been told about her fear of the *Kinshu Maru*, had been forced to content himself with only another, closer, examination of Annie O'Hare's body in the makeshift morgue that had been set up next to the ice plant. The close examination endorsed his first findings; the bumptious blonde had been knocked out, if not killed outright, by a crushing blow at the base of the skull.

"It was a blow that she couldn't have gotten in the water," North had told Kenny as he straightened up. "Whoever dealt it swung from the heels."

Cagnieri? Almost impossible. If Annie had accidentally stumbled over the fugitive soldier, Cagnieri might possibly have used his gun in his panic (if he actually had a gun) but the mutilation of the unconscious woman had been intended to make it seem that

Annie had met death by moray eels. Cagnieri would never have done that. Cross off Cagnieri as Annie O'Hare's killer.

Hugh North shifted his feet and looked down into the dark-green water. He would have given anything to have an aqualung, but if there was one on Sanga Sanga, whoever owned it was keeping it hidden; everybody he had asked had said no, there was none—how could anybody get tanks of compressed air out to this Godforsaken spot? Didn't the guided missiles use compressed air in any of their mechanisms? No.

Now Hugh told himself firmly that if Jack Flood had dived down to the wreck, if (and he had to believe she had) Annie O'Hare had made it, he could do the same. But it had been a long time since he had done any diving. He did not relish the job at hand.

He inhaled deeply several times, and with a gasp that filled his lungs to the utmost, he plunged overboard. He was on his way down through the dulling yellow-green water when the thought struck him that if Jack Flood was indeed the villain of this drama, he could have pulled a very bit of clever work by confessing that there were no morays in this lagoon when, in fact, the place teemed with them.

Eels were particularly fond of wrecks as hangouts, and inside the *Kinshu Maru* it would be very dark. It would be a hell of a thing to turn a corner on the deck of the hulk and find himself face to face with a hungry moray. But *que sera, sera,* and the wreck had to be visited.

If Flood had explored the aft section of the *Kinshu,* chances were that what he, North, was seeking was

somewhere in the forward section. *If* Flood had not
found it long before and was keeping mum about his
find. *If* Annie O'Hare had not found it just before
she died. ("Bes' li'l swimmer on Sanga Sanga, tha's
me.")

And *if* the years under water had not disposed of
the blue dog.

Oh yes, Hugh North was convinced there had been
a blue dog.

George Lee had been bound for Sanga Sanga to
recover the pearls and the microfilm from the *Kinshu
Maru.* North took that for granted, now that he knew
the story of Estelle's protests, now that Annie O'Hare
had been murdered. Lee had known the *Kinshu* was
in the lagoon, blown up as the vessel came for Esteban
Ortega and his daughter. And Lee, just before he died,
had gasped something about a blue dog's belly.

Of course (all these thoughts streaked through Hugh
North's mind as he went down, down, down into the
darkness), Lee was close to delirium if not completely
in the clutch of pain's madness, so that mention of a
blue dog's belly might have been nothing more than
a scrap phrase out of a wild nightmare. What Hugh
North was banking on, however, was that the pearls,
the film, actually had been hidden in a blue dog's
belly.

Ridiculous on the face of it, but Hugh North had
figured it out this way: The only bluish-haired breed
of dogs North had ever heard of was the Kerry blue.
If there could possibly be a Kerry blue on Sanga
Sanga, how could Lee have spent so many years in a
Chinese prison and still believe it was alive after

twelve years, even in the unlikely event the dog had been force-fed pearls and films? No dice there.

So if the blue dog was not an actual animal, it must be a blue-colored artificial dog. That could include a child's toy, but was Arnulf Hansen a man who would hide something so precious in a child's toy that would focus attention by its very incongruity? No. What else?

Well, there were the conventionalized Fo dogs of porcelain that, in old China, had stood guard over millions of Chinese sleeping rooms. Those porcelain dogs were green, yellow, vermilion—or blue. The *Kinshu Maru* had been the *Chu San*, a Chinese vessel, before it had been seized by the Japs; it could very possibly have a Fo dog aboard, the original Chinese skipper's guardian against bad dreams. Hansen could have used the Fo dog for a safe-deposit vault.

That was what he had to go on and—and there was the wreck.

She lay on her side, as Flood had said, and a great hole gaped in her side, barely visible in the gloom of these depths. The torpedo had ripped her insides out, but as North detached his flashlight and played it over the wreck he saw that the *Kinshu's* superstructure was almost undamaged, although covered with barnacles and streaming with seaweed.

The door that Flood had used as an entrance hatch hung open on the vessel's poop deck. North headed for the forward section. He paddled slowly, conserving his air, his ears feeling the depth's pressure, his knife free of its sheath, his flashlight playing carefully in his path.

He gained the side of the stricken monster and drifted up to the rail, dived a bit further until he came to a door set directly under the battered bridge of the *Kinshu*. Hansen was an important spy; it was probable that he had shared quarters with the captain of the old coaster, the best accommodations the *Kinshu* had to offer, and this door was the most likely entrance to the captain's cabin.

He reached the doorway, doubled and hauled at the knob—and fell over in a backward somersault as the door came open easily, throwing him completely off balance.

He lost a dangerous amount of precious air in an involuntary exhalation of surprise. That door should have been harder to open than that—unless Annie O'Hare had come here, too, directed by the one who had sent her to her death.

He paddled close to the opening and shone his flashlight down inside. The place was a clutter of barnacle-encrusted, slime-coated furniture and sodden rubbish. It was a tomb, too; as North shot his light into a far corner he saw the upper part of a skeleton jammed between the bulkhead and a desk that had slid with the deck's list. Hansen?

He wasted no time on the skeleton; he played his light around the cabin, his lungs beginning to complain now. He expelled a minute quantity of air to relieve the ache and then, as his lamp swept the far bulkhead, now the floor of this cabin, he saw what he was looking for.

It was a blue Fo dog, almost unrecognizable under the slime that coated it. It lay face down, and its base showed a jagged hole. Hugh North knew it was empty, but he swam down, picked up the porcelain piece, peered at the opening in its base.

There were jagged edges that shone brightly against the scum that coated the rest of the dog. Whoever had beaten Hugh North to the blue dog's belly had won the race by only a few hours, and that meant that the "winner" had been Annie O'Hare.

iv

Time to go; he would just make it to the top before the blinding weakness of suffocation claimed him. He stuck the knife back in its sheath, put the Fo dog under his arm, and kicked himself up through the doorway, on up toward the dim light of safety, far above.

He was halfway to the surface when there was the streaking swirl of a sinuous body close to him. He twisted, kicked, peered over his shoulder.

There it was, a moray eel at least fifteen feet long, with the eyes of an ill-tempered adder, a mouthful of cruel teeth, the heart of an outcast demon, the voraciousness of a starved leopard.

North dropped the blue dog, freed his knife, in one swift-flowing motion. He kicked furiously now, churning the water with a reckless expenditure of strength in the hope that the commotion would confuse the eel as it sometimes (but not always or even often) did a shark.

The eel slithered its willowy length toward him, hesitated—and drove in for the kill.

North held his slash against every screaming urge. There would be no chance of a second stab here. Let those fangs fasten on his gullet (and a moray was reputed to instinctively go for the most vital part) and all his struggling would only prolong the agony; he would be dragged down and down to his death. The eel was a shimmering blur in the uncertain light, and then its devil's mask was upon Hugh North, teeth glittering.

North cut, with a forward thrust that minimized the water's pressure against his sweep. He thrust and knew as he stabbed that he had one chance in a thousand of having the blade touch, much less cut through, that tough, slime-slicked skin. He prayed, too, and Somebody listened.

He felt the jar run up his wrist and arm to tell him that he had miraculously landed. He saw the spume of dark fluid that must be the eel's cold blood. He saw the giant moray twist into a wild series of loops, bend itself into a hideous bowknot, go coiling and writhing off into the blackness. As it disappeared, flinging itself about in its death throes, another shadow flashed onto the scene and then off, in pursuit of the stricken moray. Shark!

North's brain was filled with the hammer of exploding stars, his lungs screamed their agony, as he plodded upward, his enfeebled strokes and kicks seeming to do no more than suspend him in one spot, a place where he would struggle uselessly for all eternity. A blackness edged over the rim of his consciousness, and with it the beginnings of a blissful tranquillity he half recognized as the forerunner of drowning.

So what? He could go no farther. He had made his last kick, paddled his last stroke. This was it and who cared? Let somebody else solve the mystery of Sanga Sanga. Let somebody else find the contents of the blue dog's belly. Hugh North was tired—utterly, finally tired.

He gave up his battle and sagged in the grip of this new, persuasive, unworthy lethargy—and then strong hands gripped his arms and shoulders, two surging bodies, one on each side, propelled him upward. His head broke the surface, and there came the sweeping, cleansing, revitalizing air. Pure air, sweet air, wonderful air—and never mind that it was close to a hundred degrees hot and cursed by every man and woman who breathed it on Sanga Sanga.

v

"And now I think I've got the whole picture," Colonel North told Lieutenant Kenny Trotter. "I guess it took that little hassle with the eel to work the stupidity out of my head, but, whatever it was, I think I've got it."

"I listen, O great man," Kenny salaamed. "But dish it out to me in words of one syllable because I'm only fifteen and a half y'ars old, remember."

North scowled at his aide. "One of these days," he threatened, "I'm going to have to send you to War College for a refresher course in military courtesy and discipline, beginners' class."

"This from the lips of the man Flood and I risked

life and limb to save from the deep," said Kenny sadly. "But go on, *mon colonel.* So there are eels in the lagoon, after all; Flood lied."

"*Colonel* Flood," North said severely, "and no, he didn't lie. That was a stray moray who had to get into the act just to make things look a little worse for the C.O. Colonel Flood's unlucky that way. First, he happened to have a wife who owned a .28 and who was the motherly type when it came to baby-faced killers, and then—but that's no place to start a deduction recital."

He leaned back on the pillow Kenny had propped behind him and blew smoke at the ceiling of his room. There were a few minutes to spend before he went to the headquarters building where Flood was gathering certain persons who were connected with this case, and these spare moments could well be spent in reviewing the facts, the logical suppositions, the outright guesses. It would be good training for Kenny Trotter, and, furthermore, it would peg down Hugh North's own conclusions.

"Let's go back to the murder of George Lee in Zamboanga," he said. "Laval tried to poison Lee's drink, and Lee caught him at it. Laval shot him with a .28, got away, came back to Sanga Sanga, probably in the boat provided him by the man who hired him to kill Lee and arranged for him to break Flood's restriction order."

"Got it"—Kenny nodded—"but is there something new there?"

"Laval tried to *poison* Lee," North repeated. "That

was the original plan—the gun was to be used only in an emergency."

"Poison," Trotter said slowly. "Where did Laval get the poison? Who handled poison on Sanga Sanga?"

He waited for North to speak, and when the colonel remained silent, smiling slightly at him through his cigarette smoke, he stared and blurted, "But you can't mean Major Denver, the surgeon!"

"Why not?"

"But he wouldn't have any reason to kill Lee! He's no old-timer who's on Hansen's little roll of microfilm."

"But he could use the pearls, couldn't he?" North asked.

"The pearls—hell, I'd almost forgotten all about the pearls."

"They're good to remember," the G-2 colonel said. "I've had it hinted to me, at least, that Denver came close to doing a stretch in Leavenworth for some fast operations he tried while staying out of military service. If he hasn't got the ethics of most medical men in that department, why wouldn't he be willing to go the limit for a fortune in pearls?"

"You mean Denver hired Laval?"

"I'm pretty sure he did," Colonel North nodded. "He'd be likely to know Laval was a junkie. He might even have supplied Laval with his dope—that dispensary robbery could have been a put-up job." His face sobered. "Laval might have even gone to Denver for help with his drug problem and other things such as his deviate tendencies; you recall that Denver said he'd been more or less a father confessor to this battalion ever since the chaplain was invalided out."

"I remember. How about Cagnieri, then?"

"The way I figure it, Denver realized that a hophead in a tight spot wasn't too dependable; shut off his drugs and there'd be a squealing rat. He decided he had to get rid of Laval after the kid did his job. He needed another suspect for Laval's murder, hence Cagnieri. I can't prove this—yet—but seeing that Cagnieri and Laval were buddies, it's a good bet Cagnieri's an addict, too. Or maybe he's just off his head and Denver seized on that; he'd know Cagnieri was a confused boy if anybody would.

"What the arrangement was at the guard-mount affair, I don't know. Maybe Cagnieri was under instructions to kill me, maybe Colonel Flood. The main idea was to get Cagnieri pegged as a crazy killer. I don't doubt that Denver told Laval that the Lee job could be blamed on Cagnieri once Vince was labeled a gunman. Anyway, Cagnieri missed with his carbine. Denver got him out of the guardhouse, into the hospital, and there Cagnieri quote escaped unquote after a quote fight unquote with Denver. Denver got or dealt himself a knock on the head, Cagnieri went out the window. Denver went out the same window, rounded the corner, shot Laval, and jumped back in through the window of the hospital. Then he spread the alarm about Cagnieri. So poor Vince found himself running away from a murder he didn't do, convinced the C.O. would hang him for both the Lee and Laval jobs."

"What about Mrs. O'Hare?"

"Denver found out the pearls were in the *Kinshu Maru* at the bottom of the lagoon. He knew, too, that there were no eels in the lagoon, but he just wasn't enough of a swimmer to dive for the pearls himself without an aqualung. But Annie O'Hare was a marvelous swimmer, Annie O'Hare was adventurous by nature, Annie O'Hare got full of liquor, Annie O'Hare would do almost anything to burn up Colonel Flood. Denver played up to Annie, became one of her most indefatigable boy friends. And when she got tight last night and suggested the swimming party, Denver made his pitch."

"Annie got the pearls, then?"

North nodded. "Not long before I found the blue dog. She brought them to Denver—of course I'm just theorizing now, but don't bet your month's pay that Denver won't tell all this when the screws are put to him—Annie brought the pearls to Denver to get the split that doubtless was promised, and Denver belted her in the back of the head with something, maybe Annie's flashlight, and went for his little doctor's bag. A scalpel carved up Mrs. O'Hare, no moray eel. Then Denver towed her out into the lagoon and went back to the beach party before Flood got there. It was close timing, and luck was with Denver."

Kenny Trotter pondered his colonel's solution. Finally he looked across the bed at Hugh and said, "This is all very fine, but it leaves a lot of loose ends. How did Denver know Lee was on his way to Sanga Sanga? How did he know about the blue dog's bellyful of pearls?"

"First things first." Hugh North smiled as he un-
coiled his wide-shouldered length from the bed. "Let's
take care of Doctor Joseph Denver, Major, Medical
Corps, U.S.A., first, shall we?"

vi

The unmasking of Joe Denver was brief and complete. It happened in the office of Lieutenant Colonel
Jack Flood, crowded by the presence of every man
and woman North had connected, no matter how dis-
tantly, with the case of the blue dog's belly.

Jack Flood was there, of course, and his wife, Estelle,
Arthur and Manuela Rickerson, Mrs. Janice Coulson,
Captain Pat Keene, Major Hilton Macy, a red-eyed,
ashen-faced but sober Bottles O'Hare, and—naturally
—Joe Denver. Also present in the rear of the office was
the cavalryman-turned-latrine-orderly-and-bartender
Jimmy Mulcahey, as well as Sergeants Austin Hewett
and Marvin Butler. These were the old-timers who had
served in the Philippines before World War Two and
who, like Mulcahey, might possibly have dealt with
Hansen and his spy ring.

In the hallway and outside the window of the C.O.'s
office were armed M.P.'s, placed there by Lieutenant
Colonel Flood on advice of Colonel North.

"It's too hot to waste time," Hugh said when he took
the floor, "so we'll get right to the business at hand. If
you don't know it yet, I'll say right now that Mrs.
O'Hare was not killed by moray eels; she was murdered by somebody in this room."

There was a strangled gasp from Bottles O'Hare, and he lurched out of his chair. "Who killed her?" he cried hoarsely. "Tell me who killed her!"

"Captain, the man who did is going to pay for it," North said, the iron ring of authority clanging. "When I name him, you'll stay right where you are. Otherwise, I'll have to put you under protective arrest right now."

O'Hare subsided, his eyes guttering murkily. "Okay," he growled, "I'll stand by and watch him hang, but if the sonofabitch looks like he's gonna get off I'll take care of him."

"He won't get off," Colonel North said. He swiveled until he faced Major Denver directly.

"Denver," he said, his voice icy, "do you want to confess now or do you want me to put you through the wringer right here?"

The room rumbled and was deathly still. Joe Denver gaped unbelievingly, his face fish-belly white. "What're you talking about?" he demanded finally.

"You got Paul Laval to kill George Lee," North rapped out. "You killed Laval. You got Cagnieri to try to kill either Colonel Flood or me, and when he missed, you let him escape from the hospital in a fake fight. You killed Mrs. O'Hare and took the pearls she had brought you from the wreck of the *Kinshu Maru*."

"You're crazy!" Denver gasped.

"No, and I don't think you are, either—not crazy enough to plead insanity," Hugh said grimly. Before Denver could move, he darted to the side of the major's chair and snatched up the surgeon's medical kit.

Denver made a belated grab for his little black bag. "You've got no right to open that!" he screamed.

Hugh North did not bother to reply. Instead, he wrenched open the bag, looked down into it. What he had depended on had stood up; Joe Denver, like most killers, was an egomaniac who had thought himself so clever in his crime that he dared carry the evidence of murder about with him. He had been very sure of the sacrosanct inviolacy of a doctor's bag, and there, at the bottom of the kit, lay a moldy leather sack that bulged like a boy's bag of marbles. Beside the sack lay a .28 pistol and a waterproof flashlight that had been dented by a heavy blow, Annie O'Hare's death blow.

The scalpel Denver had used on Annie O'Hare was in the bag, too, although which one of the dozen or so that were fitted so neatly in their sockets was the actual weapon could never be established. They all glistened now, the murder weapon cleaned since Joe Denver had trotted off from the lagoon shore so solicitously with Bottles O'Hare, his victim's husband.

"You can't prove anything!" Denver was shrieking. "You've got no right to open that bag—it's illegal! Search and seizure, by God! I tell you, when a smart lawyer gets you on the stand you won't have a leg to stand on! I know my rights!"

"Shut up," North said savagely. "I've got a hundred things on you, Denver, that will lead you right to the rope or the chair or the gas chamber or wherever you're going. And if they don't work I'll see that you're turned over to Captain O'Hare—maybe you'd like to argue constitutional rights with him."

"I say you can't—oh, God!" Then Denver broke down completely, the hopeless sobs wrenching him, his words an unintelligible babble. Before the loathing,

contemptuous eyes of all in the C.O.'s office he grov-
eled, he whimpered, he made pawing grabs at that bag
with its sack of pearls, and now he was gibbering like
an idiot.

North eyed him and sighed. It would have been nice
if Joe Denver had kept his grip on himself long enough
to tell who the *real* villain was, the traitor who was to
blame for all the evil things that had happened at Fort
Winfield on Sanga Sanga.

Of course he could wait until Denver managed to
get hold of himself. Then he would talk—oh, yes indeed. Joe Denver would talk his head off if he saw that
by talking there was the slightest gleam of hope that
he could save his neck. It wouldn't save him, he never
would be promised anything but swift justice, but he
would talk. Men like Joe Denver always did.

He could wait for Denver to talk, but Hugh North
told himself that many things could happen while he
waited. Best clean up this foul mess now.

"Take him away," he told the M.P.'s who had come
into the room at Lieutenant Colonel Flood's order.
North waited as Denver was borne shrieking out of the
still, paralyzed room, and then he turned to the evil
creature who was responsible for all this.

His voice was clear, the voice of doom, as he shot
his question.

"And how about you? Do you want to carry this on
any further or do you want to come out and admit
you're the spy whose name is on Arnulf Hansen's
microfilm?"

There was a moment's silence, then the lightning
thrust of slim fingers into a handbag. North flung him-

self across the room, but as Denver had been late in reaching for his doctor's bag, Colonel Hugh North was a fraction of a second late in reaching the woman who held a gun, a lady's .28-caliber revolver, against her own breast.

There was a muffled shot, and gentle, lovely Janice Coulson half rose from her chair before she slumped forward into Hugh North's arms.

Chapter Five

HUGH NORTH entered the room he shared with Lieutenant Kenny Trotter and scaled his cap to the top of the bureau. His aide looked at his deeply lined face and held his tongue.

"She just died," North said in a dull voice. "They thought for a while that she might make it, but they were only corpsmen, after all, and they couldn't save her, though they did their best."

"Denver?" Trotter asked.

"He laughed at us when we said we'd let him out of his cell to try to keep her alive. Said we'd better not let him get close to her with a probing scalpel, and I guess he was right."

He sat down on the side of the bed and bent to run his fingers through his close-cropped hair with a sigh.

"This job," he said in a low voice, "has its bad moments. Harry Crooks' wife, and Harry loved her so."

"Did she talk before she died, sir?" Kenny asked.

"Oh yes; she seemed anxious to talk. She told us everything. It was just about the way we'd figured it, Kenny."

He lay back across the bed and stared up at the ceiling, thinking of the old days, the good days, when Janice Coulson had been Janice Crooks, the charming hostess at the party given to celebrate her husband's majority. He spent no more than two minutes surrendered to regrets, nostalgia, grief, and then he raised himself to a sitting position and reached for a cigarette.

"I hope you learned something from the mistakes I made in this case, Lieutenant," he said briskly. "In being so slow to recognize Janice Coulson as the traitor-spy I did something you must never do; I didn't go back to basics."

"Meaning?" Kenny asked.

"The spy with whom George Lee would have contact, the person who had to do anything to keep from being exposed, must have been important in the Hansen ring," North explained. "It was improbable that Hansen kept a blackmail file on the small fry; he and his gang had too many of them. If I'd recognized that fact sooner and stuck to it, I'd have eliminated most of the others right away. Flood, Rickerson, Macy, O'Hare, Keene—they were all sergeants before Pearl Harbor. They gave Lee information to get out from under the loan shark, sure, but it couldn't have been important enough to use as blackmail.

"Then who was the logical person to have been an important link in Hansen's spy ring? Estelle Flood was a young girl when Hansen was operating; she was a possible suspect but not too convincing. Manuela's *father* was important, but she had already suffered ostracism for what her father had done; why would she kill now to keep her past hidden? Because of her new husband? Yes, that would be possible, too, but Rickerson had already stuck by her in the face of every opposition; why wouldn't she expect him to do the same as regards new evidence that she had been active in her father's operations?"

"But Mrs. Coulson—"

"*Was* Mrs. Major Harry Crooks of the Army Air Corps," North finished. "*Major Crooks* had important information about planes that the Japs wanted more than anything else."

"You think this Major Crooks—"

"I *know* Harry was no spy," North cut in again. "But he was a wild one, a heavy drinker, an inveterate gambler. He was always in debt. He was careful enough about his tongue even when he was drinking, but isn't it safe to assume that he told his beloved wife things that should never have been told? With her need of money, wouldn't it be logical to assume that Janice sold her husband's information to Hansen and his agents? Wasn't Janice Coulson the only one of the four women here at Sanga Sanga—the only *person* in Fort Winfield—who *surely* had access to information that would make her important in Hansen's ring?"

"Yes," Kenny Trotter nodded. "The way you put it, it seems obvious."

"It's not that simple. Janice was clever. Take the matter of her second husband, Captain Coulson. Colonel Flood said that all the sergeants he knew swapped information for cut-down debts—except Coulson. He was an Air Corps man in those days, but he must have suspected what was going on in Flood's crowd. Obviously Coulson idolized his major's wife from a distance. Perhaps he learned something about what she was doing before Major Crooks was killed—maybe not. Janice said she wasn't sure, but she suspected that he knew, and so, to shut him up, she married him. Then she proceeded to eliminate his danger to her by driving him crazy."

His mouth thinned at the thought.

"She found a good ally in Denver when he became her lover; together they did a complete job of it on Coulson. They told Colonel Flood that Coulson had to be spurred on to the point of cruelty to save him from melancholia. Flood was fond of Coulson, he wanted to keep him active until he could retire in grade, and so he did what they said."

"And so finally she shot him," Kenny Trotter said dryly.

"Yes, she admitted that," North nodded. "Also she said that when Estelle Flood came to her with the story of Jack finding the *Kinshu Maru* in the lagoon, she knew her past had caught up with her. She had been warned by somebody in the ring that Hansen had the microfilm on him when he died. So Janice told Estelle about Hansen and said—oh, she was very concerned for poor Estelle's happiness—said that Jack Flood had dealt with Hansen's agents and therefore must have his name on that microfilm. That's why Estelle begged her husband to stay away from the wreck; Janice suggested that. You see, Janice used her big-sister role to convince Estelle that if that microfilm was unearthed, she would have to report it to headquarters; if it stayed where it was, she would do nothing out of the goodness of her heart and her love for Estelle—she'd really have no proof of anything, would she?"

"But how could Mrs. Coulson tell Estelle all this without implicating herself?" Trotter wanted to know.

"I told you she was clever, and the others trusted her implicitly; she was the only person on Sanga Sanga that they could trust and confide in. She told Estelle that her first husband knew all these things and had told her—Harry Crooks became a sort of super G-2 operative in her stories to Mrs. Flood. She could be convincing, too, in her quiet, sweet way. She had the confidence of the three other women on the island, Estelle, Manuela—even Annie O'Hare. Each came to her with her troubles, and she picked the brain of each to get what she needed to know. She used them, even while she poisoned their minds.

"In Manuela, she planted the suspicion that her husband had married her only to find out what she knew of her father's operations; Rickerson was a member of Hansen's gang, too, according to Janice's lies to Manuela. Of course it was Janice herself who spied on Manuela, went through her things, trying to find out if the girl actually *did* know anything about the Hansen ring and might point the finger at her. In Annie O'Hare, Janice put the idea that Jack Flood had killed Coulson, among other things. Every time she gave her gentle counsel she sowed suspicion and fear and hate—and all with that beautiful, sad smile.

"She was even more effective in dealing with the men. They all adored her, you know. She said Pat Keene was ready to marry her when Coulson died, and that made him easy meat for her; she kept him on the verge of throttling Flood with her lies. She used to tell Bottles O'Hare that she didn't blame him for drinking —his wife was a tramp, not good enough to touch his shoes. At the same time she was telling Annie, in her clever, oblique way, that Bottles was a stupid, selfish sot, so why not seek love someplace else? She even had Jack Flood half convinced that Estelle was following Annie's lead in playing around with enlisted men; every time Estelle did anything to make this place more bearable for the troops, Janice would be there with her subtle poison for Jack's ear.

"When Joe Denver came to Sanga Sanga, Janice recognized him at once for another of her kind, willing to do anything for a buck. Thieves—and worse— can tell each other at a mile, something like alcoholics. The two of them worked as a team."

"They sure did a good job of stirring up this garrison," Kenny murmured. "What was the idea of making all this trouble, Colonel?"

North gave his aide a disapproving stare. "You're forgetting basics, Lieutenant," he said. "Janice was an enemy agent in Manila because she was in a good position to be. And with the confidence and love she was given here, wouldn't you say she was in a good position here, too? She'd get information here in those little heart-to-heart talks that would mean a good deal to a foreign power interested in our guided-missile bases, wouldn't she? That's what she was doing; still selling out her country, breaking down morale on Sanga Sanga, right up to the end."

"Well, then," Kenny said soberly, "I don't feel sorry for her, like I've got to admit I did."

"No, never feel sorry for Janice Coulson," North said. "She could have done a lot of damage if George Lee hadn't gotten out of that Chinese Red prison. Lee communicated with her from China, telling her about the blue dog, using the old code Hansen had used—he took à chance there of a G-2 operative being in Sanga Sanga and intercepting it, but he got away with it. When Janice got that message she went to Denver. They were lovers and had been before Denver helped her cover up Coulson's murder as a suicide. He was her lover and her spy partner, and there were those lovely pearls—sure, he would do whatever she wanted in this new situation posed by Lee.

"Denver got Laval for the job of killing Lee, then got rid of Laval as we figured he did. By the way, Cagnieri was hidden out in a cave on the mountain. He was lucky; Janice admitted that Denver planned to kill Cagnieri in time and then claim self-defense. She said Denver made an addict of the poor kid, then planted the idea in his mind—helped by Laval—that Flood had called me to Sanga Sanga to arrest him. He was trying to get me with that accidental carbine shot."

He rubbed his face and yawned; it had been a long time since he had gotten a night's sleep. "Is that it?" he asked Trotter.

"I guess so," Kenny said. "Denver and Mrs. Coulson killed Creepy so they wouldn't be bothered by a husband, is that it?"

"Well, partly that, but mostly because Coulson somehow found out that his adored Janice really had been a spy in Manila. She said he threatened to expose

145

her, and she was afraid he wasn't considered quite crazy enough to have something like that be ignored, so Denver and she arranged the suicide."

"They got Annie O'Hare into their scheme so Annie would dive for the stuff on the *Kinshu Maru?*"

"No, that was a last-minute switch. Originally, Denver and Mrs. Coulson planned to get rid of Lee, then Denver would dive for the pearls and films at the right time—he'd get an aqualung sent to Zamboanga from the States and then smuggle it into Sanga Sanga as medical supplies, do not touch. But the Lee murder was botched, more or less, and then we were here and they were afraid we'd beat them to it, so when Annie got drunk last night, Janice gave Denver the word. Joe got Annie to dive, partly on a dare and partly on a promise of a split on the pearls. Annie O'Hare fairly sober was full of enough hell to go for something like that; plastered, she leaped at the chance. When she came ashore with the pearls, Denver killed her."

There was a brief silence.

"And the microfilm?" Kenny Trotter asked.

"We take that with us when we leave here," Colonel North said. "Just before she died, Janice said that she'd looked it over. Without a projector, of course, she couldn't see much, but a magnifying glass gave her some names which, she said, were going to open some official eyes mighty wide. For some reason she seemed pleased at the fact that she wouldn't be the only one to crash because of what was in the blue dog's belly."

After a brief silence, Lieutenant Trotter stirred. "You said something about leaving here," he murmured. "Just when is that, and don't say more than it takes us to pack and get the aircraft rolled out or I shall scream loudly."

"I've just come from talking to headquarters by radio," Colonel Hugh North said, his face sober. "They mentioned something about a case that needs looking into right away."

"Where?" asked Trotter joyously. "Let's go."

"Maybe you won't think so badly of this island paradise, Sanga Sanga, when you hear," North said. "This case is connected with Operation Deep Freeze, up where the temperature never gets above twenty below."

Kenny Trotter mopped his sweaty face with a handkerchief and grinned.

"I detect a barefaced lie in your voice and manner, *mon colonel*," he said, "but keep it up; I love it."